THE NAZI CONSPIRACY

SCOTT STROSAHL

ISBN: 0615581625

EAN: 978-0615581620

Foreword

dolf Hitler's final days were ones of terror and seclusion that ultimately led to the suicide of himself and his new bride, Eva Braun. On April 30, 1945, the Soviet Army was bearing down on the Führerbunker, and Hitler knew that defeat was imminent. Adolf wished to avoid suffering the same fate as his ally Mussolini, who several days earlier had been shot, then hung by his heels in Milan and posthumously beaten, stoned, and otherwise publicly humiliated. Therefore, the Führer ensured his reign would end on his terms, by a combination of cyanide and a gunshot to the head.

According to witnesses, Adolf and Eva bid farewell to their friends and retired to their quarters. About an hour later a gunshot was heard, and the couple was found dead on the sofa. The other residents of the bunker removed the bodies to a small garden above ground and lit them on fire. Soon after, the Soviets arrived and recovered what was left of the corpses. For several decades the remains were kept hidden away by the Soviet Union, and finally destroyed in 1970, save for a few pieces of bone which they preserved and put on display.

In 2009, experts at the University of Connecticut examined these remaining skull fragments and were surprised when DNA tests revealed that they came from a woman. Further tests ruled out Eva Braun as the source as well, due to the presence of a gunshot wound—Eva was reported to have poisoned herself. These findings resurfaced much of the faded skepticism around Adolf's suicide.

Later that same year, following the signing of Executive Order 13489, which repealed Executive Order 13233 and opened up records of former Presidents to the Freedom of Information Act, a previously classified document surfaced which purported to explain these inconsistencies regarding the death—or possible deception—of Adolf Hitler. As of late 2010, the whereabouts of the document's author, Caleb Scott, are unknown as he was conveniently sent out of the country on a confidential matter shortly after the document's discovery.

IV

Before leaving town, however, he recorded the events surrounding his findings so the world could know the truth. This is his story.

NSC __13__   COPY NO. __1__

A REPORT
TO THE
PRESIDENT OF THE UNITED STATES
by

CALEB SCOTT

on

THE ACTIONS OF ▮▮▮▮▮▮▮▮▮▮▮ WITH
RESPECT TO THE EXTENT OF NAZI
CONTROL OVER FOREIGN GOVERNMENTS.

August 10, 1990

WASHINGTON

Chapter 1

I t was a Friday morning around ten o'clock, and I had just begun mounting my fourth stainless steel sample for the day when a large man in a charcoal suit barged into my lab. I started at the intrusion and jumped up from my chair, knocking it over loudly.

"Are you Caleb Scott?" he demanded.

"Y...yes, why?" I stuttered. "Who are you?" I was not accustomed to having trespassers in my lab, and his use of dark sunglasses indoors unnerved me. They gave him the appearance of a person with something to hide, and I was immediately suspicious.

"Agent Smith, Secret Service," he replied, producing identification from inside his jacket. Something to hide, indeed. He offered the card to me and I crossed the room to retrieve it.

The card did in fact say Agent John Smith, but I seriously doubted that was his real name. It seemed a bit too... ordinary. I had no idea what Secret Service credentials were supposed to look like, but I studied the laminated document intently. I flipped it over a couple times and rubbed it between my fingers before hesitantly nodding my approval as if I doubted its validity. In reality, as long as it wasn't written in crayon on a napkin it was going to pass my inspection. I returned the ID to him and righted my chair.

"And what are you doing here?" I asked, motioning for him to sit in the empty seat my lab mate normally used. He ignored me and remained standing near the door. I was running through different scenarios in my head and could come up with not one possible reason why the Secret Service would want to visit me.

"The President would like to have a word with you, sir."

I frowned. "The President of what?" Surely he couldn't mean the United States.

Agent Smith just frowned right back. "Sir, you'll need to come with me. I can explain everything on the way."

"Right now?" I protested. "But I'm at work..." Not that my job was real exciting. Mounting and polishing samples for inspection was the main part of my job at McHenry Steel in Harrisburg, Pennsylvania, where I had been working for just over a year. It was pretty boring, and I felt a tremendous waste of my education. Having spent four years at Iowa State University learning everything there is to know about metallurgy, I was now resigned to looking through a microscope at chunks of metal all day long.

This tedious work was necessary in order to measure the thickness of the coatings on the metal sheets. Clients ordered the samples with different specifications for the stainless coating, and the only way to do quality control testing was to cut a piece off and physically measure it. The problem was, the thicknesses of the coatings were on a scale that could only be seen with a microscope.

But they paid me a decent wage and I had good benefits, so I kept working there with the hope that someday I could move into research and development. 'R&D' as it was called, was where I had always pictured myself—solving problems and creating new inventions—but that was a hard nut to crack, and after a year I was getting tired of the same old boring day. That is until the visit from the Secret Service.

"We've cleared it with your boss," Agent Smith assured me. "Mr. Bush would like to see you this morning."

Mr. Bush? I thought. *George Bush? Why would he want to see me? Why does he even know who I am?* I glanced around the room, trying to think of a reason to object. I drew a blank, so I just shrugged and said, "Okay, I guess."

We walked quickly down the hallway, and luckily avoided contact with most of my coworkers. I could just imagine the rumors they would start when they found out I had been escorted out of the building by the Secret Service.

"The Secret Service arrested Caleb today."

"Did you hear Caleb threatened the President?"

"I heard he was part of a conspiracy to assassinate President Bush."

Before long, it would probably show up on the local news.

I smiled and nodded to Susie, the receptionist, as she lounged lazily at her desk by the main entrance. It occurred to me that Agent Smith had probably identified himself to her when he arrived, and she would undoubtedly spread the news. However, she appeared quite disinterested as we passed, briefly lifting her hand from the desk in a sort of half wave. I followed Smith through the revolving door to a black Lincoln town car waiting outside. I motioned toward the employee lot about a hundred yards away. "What about my car?"

"Don't worry," he said with a dismissive wave of the hand. "You don't need it right now."

I was directed into the backseat, and Agent Smith took the wheel. For the next two hours we drove to Washington in silence, despite several attempts on my part to start up a conversation. Eventually I gave up, and the excitement started to wane as the silent monotony of the highway took over.

I began to think of my girlfriend Katie and her return from a business trip later in the day. Hopefully I would be back in time for our dinner. It always felt strange when I didn't see her for several days, and her homecoming was reason to celebrate. I was planning to make chicken parmesan and rent a movie. She never felt like going out to eat after a business trip since that was all she did while she was away.

We met in college and had been dating for a little over three years. She'd landed a good job in Harrisburg and was the unofficial reason I had moved to Pennsylvania after graduation. Getting a good job in the area was the official reason, but we both knew we'd probably be getting married in the near future. The main obstacle for me was saving up the money to buy a ring; paying back school loans had really eaten into my budget.

My heart resumed its hurried pace as we crossed the Theodore Roosevelt Bridge and the Lincoln Memorial came into view. Now only a few blocks from The White House, the reality of my situation began to settle in.

I was about to meet the most powerful man in the world, and he wanted to see me.

Chapter 2

I climbed out of the car and briefly stretched my legs as I took in the surroundings. To the north, a small crowd of people had gathered just outside the fence on Pennsylvania Avenue. Many were taking pictures, and it felt strange knowing that they probably thought I was someone important.

I followed Agent Smith through the large french doors at the front of the White House, and we stopped briefly at a security desk to acquire a temporary visitor pass, complete with a bad snapshot of myself attempting to smile. I struggled to keep up

THE NAZI CONSPIRACY

as he led me quickly down a maze of hallways, and I attempted to quickly admire the multitude of artwork as I passed. Although I didn't recognize the artists, let alone any of the paintings, I sensed they would probably be considered special by people who knew about such things, and it seemed only appropriate that I should take a second to observe them.

I was surprised at the number of people in the building, carrying papers and talking on phones, and all seemingly in a hurry. I began to wonder if perhaps we had been invaded or something. But surely I would have heard about that on the news, right?

Finally we came to a closed door at the end of a hallway, and Smith knocked sharply twice. From inside, a voice invited us to enter, and I suddenly found myself being escorted into the Oval Office.

I thought for sure that I was dreaming and would soon wake up to find I'd dozed off in my office again. Instead, I was greeted by none other than the 41st President of the United States, George Herbert Walker Bush. He was sitting on an ivory damask sofa to my left as I entered, and his wife, Barbara, sat opposite him on a matching sofa. They had apparently been eating lunch, as I saw several plates of partially eaten food on the table between them.

I was struck by how much larger the room was than I anticipated. I had seen pictures of course, but it was still an odd feeling standing in a room with curved walls. The furniture was arranged in a way that made it seem almost like two separate spaces. On

7

the near side, the President and First Lady reclined in what could be likened to a small living room, complete with a fireplace and coffee table. At the far end sat a large, dark, wooden desk in front of tall windows overlooking the expanse of green outside. Long blue curtains framed the windows, and formed the well-known backdrop for Presidential addresses on television.

"Caleb, my boy," the President exclaimed, as if we were old friends. "Thanks for coming." I hadn't realized that I'd had a choice. Not that I would have passed up an opportunity to see the actual White House. I had been to Washington once on a trip in high school, and we had toured "the White House". However, the tour for the public included only one small wing of the building, which was set up like a museum, containing artwork and furniture from past presidencies. The actual part that was used from day to day was off limits to visitors.

"Uh... no problem, sir," I managed, as if I was doing him a favor. Barbara gave her husband a quick smile, nodded politely in my direction, and exited through a side door, abandoning the rest of her lunch. I was directed to the couch and sat down. The President dismissed Agent Smith, who glanced wearily at me before hesitantly taking up a post in the hallway, just outside the open door and certainly within earshot. He clearly did not trust me. I was only slightly hurt by this and consoled myself with the fact that it was his job not to trust people. The president remained standing and paced the room while he spoke.

"I've had my eye on you for a while now," he began. "I was very impressed with that project you worked on for the DOD."

"Th... thank you, sir," I stammered. "It was a group effort though. I can't take all the credit." So that was how he knew who I was. A couple years earlier, while working toward my degree at Iowa State, I had assisted with a research project for one of my professors. He had received a grant from the Department of Defense to develop an explosive that would work underwater.

"That's not what Dr. Hamilton tells me. From what I hear, it was your outside the box thinking that led to the breakthrough."

"Well, he's very generous." It was true that the successful design had stemmed from a suggestion of mine, but at the time I didn't have the know-how to actually make it work. It was as if I were getting credit for inventing the wheel when I had simply suggested fewer corners.

The President nodded approvingly, apparently impressed by my modesty, although it was actually closer to embarrassment. "I asked you here today, Caleb, because I was hoping you could help me."

"I don't understand," I laughed. "What could I possibly help you with?"

"Why don't we take a walk," he suggested, glancing at the open door. "Out in the garden, we can speak more privately." I nodded my approval and he quickly exited the room, apparently expecting me to follow. I hurried out the door and into the intimidating gaze of Agent Smith. I smiled and nodded to him, eliciting an even stronger scowl, then strode hastily after the President.

I was led down another ornamented hallway that I had no time to admire, and finally out into the rose garden. It was the middle of summer and the flowers were in full bloom—a rather impressive sight and another unfortunately missed on the 'public tour'. I watched as several secret service agents took up positions around the perimeter, but we still had ample space to talk without being heard.

"What I am about to tell you is very sensitive and more than confidential," he said as we slowly traversed the garden. He glanced around as we spoke, admiring the multitude of flowers as if viewing them for the first time. To the casual observer, we were just a couple of pals out for a stroll. No one would have guessed that the most powerful man in the world was talking to a lowly quality control engineer from Iowa.

"Okay, I understand," I nodded, although in truth, I didn't understand anything that had happened so far that day.

"I hope you do, because this is beyond top secret. Well," he corrected himself, "technically there is no classification above top secret... but even members of my cabinet are in the dark on this one." He paused and turned to look at me, driving home

how serious he was. I began to wonder if I really
wanted to know what he was going to tell me. A
range of possibilities flooded my brain—government
funded human experiments, some sort of impending
global epidemic, or maybe aliens? I considered
thanking him for the car ride and the tour and bolting
for the exit, but in the end curiosity got the better of
me, and I invited him to continue.

"How much do you know about World War
II?" the President began.

"Um, just what I learned in school, I guess."
World War II? I thought. *That was over forty years ago.
Unless they have invented time travel, I doubt I can do
anything about World War II now.* Maybe the
government had been experimenting on aliens and
created a global epidemic of time traveling humans. It
was an interesting premise for a movie, but not very
plausible.

"Well, as I'm sure you already know," he
continued, "Adolf Hitler married his mistress, Eva
Braun, shortly after his 56th birthday, while hiding in a
bunker in Berlin. Less than two days later, the two of
them said their goodbyes to the other members of the
bunker and retreated to his personal study. A gun shot
was heard, and several of Adolf's staff entered the
room to find them dead on the sofa. The bodies were
removed from the bunker and lit on fire, but Soviet
shelling prevented the SS guards from completing the
cremation. A few hours later, a SMERSH team found
the remains in a shell crater..."

"Um... SMERSH, sir?" I interrupted. I was not familiar with the term.

The president looked confused, as if everyone knew about SMERSH. "Yes, SMERSH, the soviet counter intelligence group."

"Oh, yes, of course," I said, nodding as if I knew this and it had just slipped my mind. "Go on."

He wrinkled his brow, and I got the feeling he wasn't used to being interrupted. "Where was I...? Oh yes, the remains were removed from the bunker by the Soviets and an autopsy was subsequently completed, etc." He motioned with his hand making a circle in the air, indicating that the rest of the story followed and he didn't feel the need to repeat all of it. I kept nodding as if I was well aware of what happened next, when in reality I knew very little of the story. I wasn't about to tell him that though.

"Are you with me so far?" he asked.

"Sure," I nodded. Despite my lack of expertise on the subject, so far everything he'd said was nowhere near top secret, and was probably even in a text book I once owned. I was waiting for the "but", and when it came, I was not disappointed.

"But, what you don't know is that those remains were not Adolf and Eva Hitler." He paused dramatically, wanting to gauge my reaction. I opened my mouth to respond, but the connection from brain to tongue seemed to have been rerouted and nothing came out. He smiled, apparently satisfied with my silence.

I paused on the perfectly manicured path and studied some bright pink roses as I considered this revelation. After a few moments I asked the obvious question, "So, then who were they?"

He nodded approvingly. "Well, our best guess is doubles. Adolf Hitler was a very paranoid man and had several look alikes that attended all manner of events and meetings for him. For all we know, he had one for Eva as well. He could have easily poisoned and shot the doubles to fake a suicide."

As surprised as I was, I still managed to pick up on something in his explanation. "But you said 'was a very paranoid man', meaning he is in fact dead, right?"

The president nodded. "Very perceptive; I like that." I was beginning to get the feeling that he was evaluating me, almost like a teacher testing his student, but I didn't know why. "Yes, Adolf Hitler is dead. However, he did not die until October 27, in '62, and it was not a suicide." He smiled wryly and let that last statement hang out there.

"October of '62? Why does that sound familiar?" I knew it was something, but I couldn't quite place it.

"The Cuban Missile Crisis," he responded.

I nodded, remembering now that we had talked about it in a class I took in college. It was a political science class I had taken as an elective, and from what I recalled, the Cuban Missile Crisis had to do with the Soviet Union sending missiles to Cuba on large ships. We attempted to stop and inspect all ships headed for Cuba and when several of them wouldn't stop, there was a real danger of war breaking out. I didn't see what that could have to do with Adolf Hitler. "Unrelated, I assume?"

The president chuckled. "Oh, no. Quite the contrary. The Cuban Missile Crisis *was* the death of Adolf Hitler." He must have seen from my face that I was lost, so he continued.

"You see, Hitler's modus operandi during the war was to invade and control. Let's pretend that Hitler was a bank robber. He would be a 'smash and grab' kind of guy. This works for a while, but it draws so much attention that you're doomed to failure. You'll never be able to hit every bank in town—or in this case, every country. Since the fall of the Third Reich and his phony suicide, he's been trying a different technique."

"What's that?"

"He's been having his friends get jobs at all the banks and take control for him. If you're not looking for it, you won't even see it. By the time anyone catches on, it'll be too late."

I thought I was beginning to get the picture, although I wasn't sure if I believed it. "So, you're saying that Castro is a puppet for Adolf Hitler?"

"Essentially," he nodded. "The Soviets weren't sending missiles into Cuba to launch against us. They were after the same thing we were—Adolf Hitler. The KGB had some reliable intel putting

Hitler on a freighter departing Milan that was bound for Cuba. We had suspected for a while that he was behind the installation of Castro as Prime Minister, and the Soviets confirmed our suspicions. Khrushchev and Kennedy set up the whole missile fiasco as a cover for a joint assassination operation. The Cold War was temporarily halted as we worked together on something larger."

"So, the assassination was successful?" I asked.

"Yes," he nodded. "Navy seals boarded the freighter and after an exhaustive search, found him in a hidden compartment below deck."

"And in the meantime, the American people were scared to death that a nuclear holocaust was imminent," I retorted, surprised at my own frankness with the President.

"True," he said with a sigh, "but sometimes deception is necessary."

I acknowledged this unfortunate fact with a slight nod, and he decided to continue. "For the next year, we and the Soviets thought that was the end of it... until November 22, 1963."

I frowned because I knew that date. "President Kennedy's assassination?" I asked. He nodded.

As I thought about this, I remembered seeing a TV special about Kennedy assassination conspiracy theories on Dateline, or 60 Minutes, or some similar show. As I recalled, one of them involved Lee Harvey Oswald being hired by Castro to kill Kennedy.

According to the paranoid nut jobs they had interviewed, the CIA had made several unsuccessful attempts at Castro's life, and this was his retaliation. In 1968, then-President Johnson had even told a reporter, "Kennedy was trying to get to Castro, but Castro got to him first." I assumed now there must be more to the story.

"So, Castro had Kennedy killed in retaliation for the assassination of Hitler?" I speculated, thinking I sounded a bit like a nut job myself.

"Basically. But it didn't end there. It seems someone was still pulling the strings behind Premier Castro."

"Don't tell me we got another double on the ship," I said.

"No, no," he replied. "That was him. We believe somebody stepped in to take his place."

"So, the organization lives on," I said, more to myself then to him. I wasn't sure if I believed everything I was hearing. It all sounded like one of those conspiracy theories that crazy people come up with. But this was the President of the United States. Surely he was somewhat reliable, wasn't he?

"Yes, we're pretty sure."

"Pretty sure?"

He shrugged. "About 95%." We reached the other side of the garden and paused before getting too close to any of the secret service loitering on the sidewalk. I turned to face him and said, "Mr. President, I don't understand. Clearly this is not something that everyone knows about." I motioned to the agents all around us that he obviously did not want listening in. "Why are you telling me?"

He gave me his politician smile. "Because I want you to do something for me."

"Me do something for you? What could you possibly want from me?" I laughed, but he didn't, and I realized he was serious.

"Son, you're going to do a little snooping for me," he said matter of factly. I wasn't sure what "snooping" meant, but luckily he continued. "Obviously you're very smart, and I think you are just what we need for this operation."

I started to shake my head and held up my hands in protest. "Sir, I appreciate the compliment, but I don't think I'm the right guy. Surely there are people at the CIA, or NSA, or some other acronym that would be better."

"I already have a whole team in place," he acknowledged. *Great, then what am I here for?* I wanted to say. "I need someone who..." he hesitated, looking for the right words, "who is unencumbered by outside influences and has an unbiased view of the situation. You'll be going somewhere warm. Think of it as a vacation."

I searched for an excuse. "You know, I don't really have much vacation time right now..."

He interrupted me with a dismissive wave of the hand. "Already taken care of," he said.

"What do you mean?"

"I had you fired," he replied nonchalantly, as if it was something he did every day.

"You what?" I exclaimed. Even if I didn't enjoy my job, the security of a steady paycheck and benefits was not something I was eager to lose.

"Don't worry," he said, placing a hand on my shoulder. "When you return you'll be happily employed again."

"Return from where?"

"I'm sending you on a little field trip," he explained. "You leave in an hour from Dulles."

"An hour?" I thought of the dinner I had planned with Katie.

"Don't worry about packing," The President instructed. "Everything you need will be on the plane. You'll be back in no time."

"And then you'll get me my job back?"

"Your job won't be an issue. Everything will be taken care of." He was using his politician smile again. I considered my options for a moment. On the one hand, I wasn't really the adventurous type and I knew squat about 'snooping'. On the other hand, my job was boring, and I could use a short vacation, and surely he wasn't sending me into any sort of military situation. They had Marines and the Delta Force for that. And my biggest weakness was curiosity. I always wanted to know what was going on, and what he had told me so far definitely piqued my interest. For some reason, he'd chosen me to do this, so I decided I would take advantage of that.

"I want a hundred grand," I blurted out suddenly, not sure what I was doing. For a split second I thought I saw surprise on his face, but he recovered quickly and nodded as if he was expecting this.

"Done," he said.

"And I don't want to be taxed on it either," I pressed. "I want a hundred grand, tax free."

He laughed. "Not a problem. Of course, you understand we can't put anything in writing."

I nodded. "I guess I'll just have to trust you then."

"I guess so." He offered his hand and I shook it. That was that.

"So, where is it that you're sending me?" I asked.

He hesitated. "You'll get all the details on the plane this afternoon. Don't worry, I'm sending one of my best men with you. Just be at Dulles Airport, hanger thirteen by 1:30."

He turned to walk away, and I started to get cold feet. "Well, I don't have a passport, so I hope it's not out of the country," I said, making one last attempt at getting out of whatever it was I had just gotten myself into.

"1:30, hanger thirteen," he said over his shoulder and then disappeared into the building.

Chapter 3

A dark haired, rough looking agent crossed the garden and escorted me around the building. He was a big guy—lots of shoulders and no neck—and looked like a fullback who had been forced to wear a nice suit for a fancy party.

"It's gotta be hot out here in that suit, huh?" I said, trying to break the silence. It was the beginning of August and even at midday the temperature was already pushing ninety-five degrees. He responded with only a shrug, as if he didn't want to lie and pretend it wasn't bothering him but didn't want to complain either.

We strolled briskly down the long driveway toward the front gate, and I began to wonder how I was expected to get to the airport. The town car I had arrived in was still sitting in front of the building, and we were now walking away from it.

"So, is someone going to be driving me to the airport then, or what?" I asked.

"Your transportation is waiting on the street," he replied without turning to look at me. I wasn't really sure what this meant, but at least I probably wouldn't be hitchhiking across town.

At the end of the driveway, he spoke briefly to a security guard at the gate, and the heavy iron bars swung open. I thanked the agent for his assistance, and he responded with a curt nod as he hiked back up the path toward the building.

I stepped through the opening and glanced around Pennsylvania Avenue. There were several cars parked along the street, but all of them were empty. As far as I could tell, there was no transportation 'waiting on the street'. I turned back to ask the guard for assistance as the gate clanged shut.

He knew about as much as I did, but offered the use of a phone to call a cab. I begrudgingly agreed, and he passed the handset through the bars as he dialed for me. I listened to the familiar beeps of numbers being punched, when I noticed something odd. Sitting next to the curb was a blue grand prix that looked almost exactly like the one I owned. *If only that were my car,* I thought, *I might make it to the airport on time.* But of course, my car was still sitting in the parking lot at work, back in Pennsylvania. Agent Smith had assured me that I didn't "need it right now."

As the phone began to ring, I noticed an 'Iowa State Alum' sticker in the back window. *What are the odds?* I thought. Someone with the same car and sticker as me happened to be parked in... Then it hit me—I was looking at my car. I lowered the handset from my face absentmindedly and looked around for some sort of explanation. I felt like I had just watched a magician pull a rabbit out of his hat, and I was trying to find the secret pocket inside that explained the impossible.

Still not believing what my eyes were telling me, I handed the phone back through the gate and walked slowly around the car to the driver's side. I gently lifted the handle, thinking the car might explode on me, and the door creaked opened. I slid inside and knew at once it was, in fact, my car when I saw the keys hanging in the ignition. I decided to accept the clever trick for what it was and move on. Surely I would have time to ponder the mystery on the plane.

While driving through the midday traffic, I searched for a payphone. After several blocks, I spotted one in a grocery store parking lot and made a hasty turn off of the roadway, prompting honks from behind. I got Katie's machine and left her a message explaining that I would have to postpone the dinner as

I was going out of town on business. I did not give any details, but told her that this was a big opportunity to make a lot of money. I would be back soon and would call her again when I could.

I felt an incredible urge to tell her everything I had just learned, but knew better. In my experience, a secret is like a hot potato. You want to toss it to someone else as soon as you get it, and the longer you hold onto it, the more it burns. But I knew this was one secret I had to hold onto, at least for now. Although I was upset over being fired, and unsure of what I had gotten myself into, there was a part of me that was excited for something different and interesting.

And of course, the money didn't hurt.

Chapter 4

Twenty minutes later, I zipped into the parking ramp at Dulles Airport with little time to spare. The clerk asked me how long I would be leaving my car with them. I impatiently explained that I didn't really know, and he looked at me like I was an idiot.

"Well, when is your return flight?" he inquired, rolling his eyes.

"I don't have a return flight," I shot back, just as condescendingly. I was in a hurry and didn't have time to deal with this.

"Well, I have to put something down on the sheet here," he motioned to the clipboard in his hand, "so we know when we can tow the car."

I sighed. "What's the longest I'm allowed to keep it here?"

"A month."

"Alright," I nodded. "Put me down for a month." I figured with a hundred grand I could afford a month's worth of parking at the airport.

He studied me for a moment and then decided I wasn't kidding and made some notes on his clipboard. He finally produced a ticket for me, which I tossed on the dash of my car as I hunted for an open space in the ramp. I eventually found one on the sixth floor, and squeezed my car in next to a van that had managed to angle park itself enough to technically be in three spaces. Walking to the elevator, I realized I was high enough to see many of the planes sitting at the hangars, and I briefly searched for number thirteen. From a distance, I could only make out the numbers on hangars three, four, and five, and I wondered which of the other dozens of jets was waiting for me.

I abandoned the search and made my way down to the first floor and into the terminal. Being unfamiliar with the layout of that particular airport, I approached the info desk and asked for directions to hangar thirteen. An overweight woman in a uniform that had clearly been designed for the less rotund informed me that I would need to check my bags with the airline, and then they would direct me to the correct gate. I explained that I was not flying with an airline and that a government jet should be waiting for me. I was then told that I would still need to check my bags, and when I said I didn't have any, she gave me the once over with her eyes as if not having luggage meant I was a terrorist. Finally, she relented and pointed me to a hallway that "should" get me where I was going.

After several minutes of searching, and two wrong turns, I found hangar thirteen and noticed a Mexicana Airlines Boeing 727 waiting outside the window. I thought at first that I must have made a mistake, but as I looked around for help, a scruffy, middle-aged man in a ball cap and a Hawaiian shirt approached me with his hand outstretched.

"Caleb Scott?" he asked, but didn't wait for a response. "My name's Solomon." A camera hung form his neck, and he looked like a tourist returning from Disney World with his wife and kids.

I shook his waiting hand. "Solomon? You mean like King Solomon?"

"Yup," he smiled. "Everyone calls me Sully."

"Alright, Sully. Got a last name?"

"Nope," he replied. Great, more mystery.

"Okay... So, where are we going?"

"All in good time, my friend. Right now, we need to board." So, now I was his friend already? He motioned toward the gate, and I saw that we were apparently getting on the Mexicana plane.

I hesitated. "Um, I don't have a passport."

"Yes, you do," he said, handing me a small blue book. Inside, I found my name and the picture they had taken earlier in the day at the White House security desk. I realized that I probably shouldn't have been surprised by this, but it seemed to make the whole thing more real for me. I was actually being sent out of the country by people who had the power to get me a passport within a few hours and without my permission.

"And we're going to... Mexico?" I asked hesitantly, looking out the large windows at the plane.

"That's one of our destinations," he replied cryptically. I waited for him to explain, but instead he simply turned and walked toward the gate, motioning for me to follow.

Once on board, I found that the aircraft was empty apart from Sully and myself. It felt strange stepping onto such a large plane filled with empty seats—almost as if I were in a museum. We found spots near the front in first class—an area of the plane I had never experienced before—and Sully pulled a large brown duffle bag out of the overhead compartment. It looked like a smaller version of the ones I always saw military guys carrying in the movies. He tossed it at my feet and directed me to the restroom to change. I glanced out the window and could see we were taxiing onto the runway.

"Aren't we going to be taking off soon?" I asked. He shrugged and looked at me blankly, apparently not concerned about walking around during takeoff. I sighed and shook my head, quickly realizing that my objections would fall on deaf ears. I walked down the aisle to the restroom just outside the cockpit and caught myself checking the latch to see if it was vacant. I chuckled as I realized how stupid that was. Of course it wasn't occupied; there were only two passengers on the plane.

Inside the small room, I opened the bag and found some jeans and a white dress shirt of some sort. It had four pockets on the front—two at the top and two at the bottom with pleats running vertically on either side of the buttons through the pockets. I struggled to change clothes in the cramped space and decided to search the rest of the bag while I was alone.

I found another passport, this one dark green with the words "PASAPORTE" and "ESTADOS UNIDOS MEXICANOS" on the front. I opened it, unsure if I actually wanted to see what was inside. As I feared, it contained the same security photo that I had found on my other passport, along with the name "Marcos Espinoza." I set this aside and continued my search, producing a brown paper bag with the top rolled down to close the opening. It was clear from the thickness of the package that there was something inside.

I unrolled the top and extracted a modest stack of cash. Flipping through, I could see they were all twenties. I estimated that it was at least a couple thousand dollars. Having all that cash made me feel like a drug dealer, and I wondered not for the first time what I had gotten myself into. Returning to the bag, I found two more paper sacks full of money—one with Mexican pesos and the other with Cuban pesos. So, we were going to Cuba.

I stared at myself in the mirror. Was I really doing this? Just a few hours earlier, I'd been bored out of my mind doing the same repetitive job I did every day. But now, I was going to be sneaking into another country with forged documents to spy on some unknown Nazi. My stomach was doing cartwheels, and little beads of sweat began to form on my forehead.

Fearing that I might be on the verge of a panic attack, I ran some water in the sink and splashed it on my face. Unfortunately, the pilot had just received permission to take off, and the plane lurched forward down the runway, causing a good portion of the water to slide out of my cupped hands and down my shirt, somehow managing to hit all four of the pockets. I was already under a good deal of stress, and what would normally be a minor inconvenience pushed me over the edge.

I pounded my fist on the sink and looked for something breakable to throw at a wall. Of course, there was nothing in the claustrophobic bathroom, so I decided to take out my anger on the mirror. However, as I balled my hand into a fist and swore at the pilot, I realized the sudden anger had calmed my stomach. It was hard to be nervous when I was upset.

As I paused to consider this revelation, my anger waned, and I had to admit how ridiculous I was acting. So what if I didn't know where I was going or what I would be doing there? It was an adventure, and one I was getting paid for. I couldn't let my emotions get the better of me and hinder my "snooping" abilities that I had yet to try out.

As I felt the plane lift into the air, I heard my dad's voice quoting scripture to my mom, "Who by worrying can add a single hour to his life?" She was an expert worrier, and I'd heard my dad quote similar verses many times in an unsuccessful effort to ease her fears. I laughed as I thought about how freaked out she would be if she knew where I was headed at that moment.

I returned the money and my old clothes to the bag before returning to my seat. Sully was reclining with his eyes closed in one of the large comfortable first class seats. He had changed his clothes as well and was wearing a white t-shirt with blue lettering that said 'Almendares' above a picture of a scorpion.

I thought he might be asleep, but I didn't really care. I had questions, and I wanted answers. I made a little stumbling motion and bumped his leg across the aisle with my knee as I sat down. He lifted his head slightly and looked at me questioningly.

"Oh good, your awake. I kinda spilled some water on whatever this shirt is," I said, turning so he could see the wet front.

"It's a guayabera and don't worry about it." He returned his head to its resting spot and closed his eyes again.

"A what?" I asked.

"A guayabera. They're common in Mexico. You've got to look like a local," he explained.

"Since I'll be flying to Cuba as a Mexican national," I stated. "A Mr. Espinoza?"

He sat up a little in his seat and turned to face me. "That's right. I guess you found your new passport."

"Yeah, and the money." I pointed at his shirt. "What's Almendares?"

He looked down as if he had forgotten what he was wearing. "Oh. It used to be a baseball team before Castro took over and banned professional baseball in Cuba. They were the scorpions," he explained, pointing at the picture on his shirt.

I nodded, and then hesitated before jumping into my next question. "So... I assume you know what I now know about Castro...?" I wanted to see if he was part of the club, so to speak, but I didn't want to give anything up in case he wasn't.

He smiled. "You mean that he's a dirt bag dictator who claims he doesn't like dictatorships? Or the fact that he was put into power by Adolf Hitler?" So, he was in the club.

"Okay, I was just checking. The president made it clear to me that this was a very closely guarded secret, so I wasn't sure who knew."

"Yeah, I know," he said, leaning back and closing his eyes again. "I know everything." He said this somberly, and I wondered if he was tired of holding the potato.

"We need some sort of password or secret handshake or something, so we know who we can talk to," I laughed. He sat up quickly with a concerned look on his face.

"You mean he didn't show you the handshake?"

"What?" I asked, a bit taken aback.

He sighed in frustration. "He always forgets the handshake. Here, let me show you," he said intently, offering his open palm. I studied him for a second and when he nodded at his outstretched hand, I offered him mine. He grasped it to shake, but slid his middle and pinky fingers to the outside of my hand so that our hands were interlocked in a sort of weaving pattern. "I call it the Hilter," he said as we shook, "although officially it doesn't have a name."

"The Hilter," I repeated, still not sure if I believed him. He removed his hand and returned to his reclined position.

"You're kidding right?" I finally said.

"Yes," he replied without opening his eyes, "and you need to be less gullible."

I sighed. "So, why are we going to Cuba? Is that where Hitler's successor is operating out of?"

"Probably not anymore, but that's the last place we're sure he's been, so that's where we'll start."

"And what is it that we're supposed to be doing there?" My mouth kept looking for answers, even though my brain was arguing that it would be best to remain ignorant.

He shrugged. "We'll see. Whatever we gotta do to find out what's going on."

"Uh huh," I wasn't satisfied. "So, you know I don't do, like missions and stuff, right? I mean, I'm not a secret agent, or whatever you guys call it."

He smiled. "Don't worry about it. Now get some rest. We've got a couple hours."

Chapter 5

y shirt was mostly dry by the time we deplaned at the Benito Juarez International Airport, also known as the Mexico City International Airport. I hefted my new bag up over my shoulder and followed Sully quickly down the terminal. Thankfully the overhead signs were printed in English as well as Spanish, so I didn't have to worry about translation.

We navigated through the crowded walkways and sat down in the hard black seats outside gate F. As we waited to board another plane, Sully directed me to my bag, where I found the plane ticket after a couple minutes of digging. I saw it also had the name

"Marcos Espinoza", and I took that as confirmation that I would be using my second new passport of the day.

"You know Spanish, right?" he asked.

"Um, not really," I replied. "I took it in high school, but I don't think I know enough to carry on a conversation or anything. I can ask for directions to the library or the bathroom. And Sesame Street taught me how to count to ten."

He frowned and made a little half sigh, half groan in frustration. "Well, just don't talk then. I'll take care of it." He studied me for a moment and then declared, "This is your first time, isn't it?"

"First time for what?"

"One of the field trips," he said. Apparently that was supposed to mean something to me.

"Field trips?" I asked.

"How new are you?" he exclaimed. I just shrugged. Clearly I was out of the loop. "You did go through the orientation, right?" he asked.

"Orientation?" I was lost. "For what?" Sully sighed again and leaned forward with his head in his hands. He rubbed his temples gently with his index fingers.

"You have no idea what you've been recruited for, do you?" he said, finally.

"I met with President Bush this morning and he said he wanted me to do some snooping for him," I explained. "Then I was taken to the airport and met you. That's all I know."

Sully sat up and turned to look at me. "You just talked to him for the first time this morning?"

"Yeah, why?"

He shook his head. "Why am I not surprised?"

He glanced around to make sure no one was listening. Only five other people were waiting at the gate, and they all sat well away from us. I assumed Sully had picked these seats for just that reason. A young couple held hands near the large windows overlooking the runway—probably newlyweds. Sitting near the television suspended from the ceiling, an Asian woman lounged lazily with her two preteen kids. None of them seemed the least bit interested in us.

"Back in 1932, President Hoover created a small group of intellectuals to solve problems," he explained in a hushed voice.

"Like a think tank," I offered.

"Yeah, basically. Sort of an unofficial cabinet. No one knew about them except himself and certain upper level people. He kept the group a secret to prevent any outside influence. You see, cabinet positions are often given to pay back favors, or to satisfy some lobbying organization, etc. But this secret group was made of unbiased, uninfluenced, intelligent people who could actually solve problems. Hoover was in Harding and Coolidge's cabinets and saw firsthand how they failed to create real solutions and give practical advice to the president.

"Hoover was an engineer and appreciated the power of a logical mind. The think tank helped him create several programs to facilitate economic recovery after the stock market crash, but his defeat by Roosevelt later in the year prevented many of them from being implemented. Roosevelt was not as keen on the idea and dissolved the group before it really got started."

"So, who got it started again?" I asked.

"Hoover continued the group in the private sector for several years before handing it off to Truman when he became Vice President in 1944. Truman had become involved with Hoover's group while creating his 'Truman Committee' to expose fraud and mismanagement in the military during World War II."

"And then Truman brought the group back to office of the president."

"Right," he nodded. "When Truman took over the presidency in 1945, the 'unofficial cabinet' moved back to the federal payroll. This transition happened at the best possible time as Hoover and Truman had the group working on a very important project."

Sully paused and looked at me, apparently expecting me to guess. I was still trying to process everything I was learning and couldn't come up with an answer. When he saw I was at a loss, he prompted me.

"Ever heard of the Manhattan Project?"

"Of course," I replied. The Manhattan Project was a secret group that had developed the nuclear weapons dropped on Japan at the end of World War II. "Are you saying that was Hoover's group?"

"The start of it, yes," he explained. "Oppenheimer, the physicist who directed the project, was a member of Hoover's initial committee. The uranium metal produced for the bombs came from a laboratory at Iowa State University, not too far from Hoover's childhood home in West Branch, Iowa."

I had done my undergrad at Iowa State, and I remembered now the stories students had told about the tunnel system between many of the science buildings. There were several underground passageways running beneath the streets and parking lots that connected the basements. Some of them were still in use, although access was limited, and were often employed by staff on cold, snowy winter days. The urban legends said that the tunnels were initially built to prevent aerial spying of the work done there by the members of the Manhattan Project.

I shook my head in disbelief. "Now you're gonna to tell me that Einstein was on the committee?"

"Of course not," he laughed. "He was German. No way they were letting him in the circle. Sure he was involved with the Manhattan Project to an extent, but not with Hoover and Truman directly." I nodded slowly. It all seemed to make sense in a strange way. I certainly was no authority on the matter.

I was about to steer him back to the topic of the "field trips" when an elderly Hispanic man hobbled past us and collapsed in a seat nearby. His whole body looked tired. His hunched back seemed ready to drop his head and shoulders forward onto the ground, and his drooping eyelids barely permitted his eyes a glimpse of the dirty floor his feet shuffled across. I glanced around the waiting area and noticed several more people had sat down while Sully was talking, but this was the first anyone had been within earshot.

I suspected the forest of gray hairs growing out of the old man's ears probably prevented him from hearing us, but Sully wasn't going to take any chances. He turned away from me and began to dig in his bag. "Tienes tu pasaporte?" he asked in Spanish. The change in language surprised me, and I struggled to comprehend what he was saying. He repeated the question as he retrieved a Mexican passport from his bag.

"Ah," I replied. "Pasaporte. Sí." I held up the dark green booklet emblazoned with the Mexican coat of arms. He nodded approvingly. From the overhead loudspeaker I heard a woman's voice rattle off a string of Spanish that I didn't catch.

Sully stood and motioned for me to follow. "Vámanos." From the number of people who also 'vámanosed' toward the petit flight attendant waiting impatiently at the gate, I assumed that we would not have the plane to ourselves on this trip.

SCOTT STROSAHL

Standing in line, I glanced out the window at a large white jet with blue and red stripes on the tail. Along the fuselage the word "CUBANA" was printed in dark blue. Seeing the word finally forced me to grasp the reality of my current situation. I was about to use a fake passport to board a plane in one of the most dangerous cities in North America and fly to a country that had, at best, little cooperation with the United States.

My heart began to race and I could feel myself beginning to panic again. What if they found out that I wasn't who I was claiming to be? Could they tell my passport was fake? I had never seen a Mexican passport before. Was that really what they looked like? I glanced around erratically for an exit or someplace to escape to. I hadn't done anything illegal yet, right? I had flown to Mexico using a passport issued to me by the U.S. government. That was technically true. If I got out now, maybe I'd still be okay. I could fake a stomach flu and hide in the bathroom until...

As if sensing my uneasiness behind him, Sully turned around and smiled calmly. "No te preocupes," he said jovily. "Todo está bien." I knew the last part meant "everything is okay", and I guessed that 'preocupes' had something to do with being preoccupied or worried, but I was too 'preocuped' with finding an exit to ask for a translation. He reached out and gently grabbed my wrist as if to comfort me. Then his grip tightened, and he began to twist ever so

40

ɘ to notice, but probably
His stare turned cold and
Don't try anything or you'll

ı abandoned my search for a way
.to the aircraft that would lead me to
and excitement, than I had ever
ɘfore.

Chapter 6

Stepping off the plane at the José Martí International Airport in Havana, I was surprised by the mild weather. My image of Cuba in July had always been one of suffocating heat, but now that I was there, it didn't seem much worse than the summers back home in Iowa. Although it was quite humid, the cool ocean breeze seemed to keep us from overheating.

It felt good to stretch my legs after sitting in a cramped seat for over two hours, and I paused briefly in the terminal to take in the sight. Sully would not allow me any time to relax, however, as he barked orders in Spanish that I mostly didn't understand. I just nodded, threw my bag over my shoulder, and followed him out to the parking ramp. He seemed to be in a hurry, and I had a hard time keeping up with him. As we crossed the street from the terminal to the parking structure, it occurred to me that I hadn't even needed to use my passport, and all my fears had been for nothing.

We hiked up the stairs to the third level— there was no elevator that I could see—and went directly to a small tan Pontiac Grand Prix with several conspicuous dents along the driver's side. Sully reached into an outside pocket on his bag and produced a set of keys, unlocking the trunk so we could deposit our luggage before climbing up front. I had ceased being surprised by anything Sully did at this point, and chalked up his possession of the keys as another mystery that would probably never be explained. Once we were inside the car and the doors had been shut, I felt it was probably safe to speak English again.

"Alright, so what's with the 'field trips'?" I asked. He chuckled and shook his head, apparently amused by my persistence. He started the car and headed down the ramp toward the exit as he finished the story we'd begun several hours earlier in Mexico.

"So, as I was saying, this group got a fresh start in a big way with the Manhattan Project. Ever since, we've been run by the highest level of the executive branch under the code name 'The Committee'."

43

"And you are a part of this group?" I asked.

He nodded. "How do you think I know so much about it?" I shrugged. I didn't think I was in any position to make assumptions about what he should or should not know.

"So, what are you, like some kind of spy or something?" I asked, trying to picture him in a tuxedo, swirling a martini. The image, however, failed to materialize as the closest I could get was cargo pants with a mug of beer.

He winced at the term. "Spies are CIA thugs," he corrected.

"And which acronym is The Committee affiliated with?"

"We're not. We get our orders directly from the President and our funding through various creative accounting techniques. It's really kind of up to the President how he wants to do it—each one has his own method."

"Creative accounting?" I asked.

"Well, you can't just add a secret organization to the federal payroll; congressmen will start asking questions. So, you find money here and there that no one will realize is missing."

"And where would one find this sort of thing?"

"Well, for example, artwork has been a popular method recently. Each president gets to decorate the White House how he pleases, so he finds an artist he likes and approaches them about commissioning a piece for the White House. The artist will do this for free of course, because it is a huge publicity boost. The President tells the artist that in order to help them out, he will report the sale at some high dollar amount, showing just how strongly he feels about the artwork."

"So," I interjected, "the accountants think the President is getting reimbursed for the painting, and the artist thinks the report of money changing hands is just for show."

He nodded. "Exactly."

"So, he steals the money from the taxpayers."

Sully grimaced. "Well, that's a bit harsh. I mean by the same logic, you could say all taxes are stolen from the taxpayers in order to provide them with services."

I nodded slowly. "Yeah, I suppose." I decided to reserve judgment until I knew more about what this mysterious group actually did for the country. "So, I still don't know what these field trips are..." I prompted.

"Well, somewhere along the way—even before my time—members of The Committee began traveling to where the problem was, in order to better assess the situation. It made more sense than meeting in a room in D.C. and relying on information that may or may not be accurate. We still left the military work to the military, but some things required more... finesse—a little less brute force and a bit more intelligence and planning."

We drove in silence through the neglected streets of Havana for several minutes as I considered this. We passed a house with a large hole in one of the walls and I wondered how much purloined cash had been spent just to sneak me into a country that was so poor. Suddenly, I was jolted out of my daydream my peripheral view caught a large object careening toward me out of an alley before it crashed into the window inches from my head. I ducked down under the dash thinking we were under attack, but quickly sat back up as Sully erupted in a fit of laughter.

I glared angrily at him and glanced back to see two barefoot boys retrieving their soccer ball from the street. As embarrassed as I was, I was mostly just relieved that I wasn't actually about to die.

"So, you think the President wants me to join The Committee?" I asked, hoping he'd forget about my overreaction.

"No," he laughed, "he doesn't want you to join. You're already on The Committee. You just haven't accepted the fact yet."

I frowned. "I never agreed to anything. He simply asked me to go to Cuba with you and do some 'snooping'. Aside from that, I've made no commitment."

Sully shrugged. "You will. Trust me." I didn't appreciate his arrogance at thinking he could predict what I was going to do.

"You don't know that," I shot back. "We've just met. You don't know anything about me."

He glanced over briefly with a little smirk, and then back to the road. "Okay," he nodded. "Let's see... Caleb Scott. Born April 13, 1967 in Des Moines, IA. Had to be hospitalized at age two months for spinal meningitis—quite serious, but no long term effects. Father was a math professor at the local college. In high school, you were a drummer in the marching band, on the swim team, and played baseball—a catcher, I believe." I began to shrink back into the seat as he managed to embarrass me yet again. But he wasn't even done yet.

"B.S. in metallurgical engineering two years ago from Iowa State University, then moved to Pennsylvania to be near your girlfriend. Went to work for McHenry Steel last year, where you sit in a laboratory looking at little pieces of metal all day—real exciting stuff, by the way. In addition to drums, you play piano, and you belong to the Lutheran church. Oh, and you're color blind."

I was staring at him and realized suddenly that my mouth was hanging open. Everything he'd said was correct. The school stuff would have been easy to find out, but the fact that he knew that I was color blind meant someone had done their homework. He glanced over at me again, smiling smugly.

"Did I forget anything?" he teased. I conceded the point and turned my attention back to the sights. It wasn't every day that I found myself driving around the streets of Havana with a secret agent of sorts in a mysterious vehicle.

Havana looked pretty much like I had expected, with lots of overhanging balconies extending out from aging buildings. Many of the roads were in sad need of repair, and I saw more than one pothole that looked like it could swallow an entire vehicle. I was surprised, however, by the number of old American cars we passed while traversing the narrow streets.

"Alright, Mr. Omniscient," I mocked, "maybe you can tell me why the President picked me."

"He didn't."

"What do you mean?"

"I did."

"You did?"

"Yes."

I started to protest that he didn't even know me, but caught myself. "Okay, then why did *you* pick me?" I asked instead.

He shrugged. "You were recommended by a friend of mine."

"A friend of yours knows me? Who?"

"You remember Alan Hamilton?"

"Dr. Hamilton? Of course. He was one of my professors at Iowa State." Dr. Alan Hamilton was the head of the underwater explosives project I had worked on. That explained why the President had been talking to him. But what I still didn't understand was how he knew someone like Sully. "So, he's a friend of yours?"

"Yup. We used to work together."

"You worked at Iowa State?" I asked.

Sully laughed loudly. "No, no. Teaching didn't used to be his only job."

I thought I knew what he was implying, though I couldn't believe it. "Are you saying... Dr. Hamilton is part of the committee?"

Sully nodded. "Yup. He doesn't travel with us anymore though. But he does consult occasionally."

I recalled a conversation we'd had one time about the Manhattan Project. Someone in class had done the math and figured out that Dr. Hamilton would have been a student at the university at the time.

"That must have been pretty exciting," she had asked.

"Not really," Hamilton responded. "I didn't even know anything was going on. None of us did. It was just the typical college year as far as we were concerned." I wondered now if he had been entirely honest with us.

Sully turned a corner, and it appeared we were leaving downtown and journeying into a residential area. I frowned at my companion. "I think I've been fairly cooperative so far with all this mystery, but I don't like being kept in the dark. You wanna fill me in on where we are going, and what we are really doing in Cuba?"

He nodded, acknowledging the validity of the query. "How much did George tell you?" he asked.

"George?"

Sully rolled his eyes. "George Bush? The President?"

"Oh, right," I said quickly. The use of the Commander in Chief's first name had caught me off guard. "Well, he explained the basics. Hitler didn't really die. He is the real power behind Castro. We finally killed Hitler in a joint effort with the Soviets that was covered up as the Cuban missile crisis."

"Joint effort my ass," he snorted. "All the Soviets did was provide us with the intel. They told us what boat he was on, and we did the dirty work." I wasn't sure if he meant 'we' as in the United States, or if he was actually there and had participated in the assassination. I got the impression it was the latter, even if he did say that "we leave the military work to the military."

"But anyway, you're right," he continued. "Except we think the organization is still working behind the scenes; that someone else stepped in to take his place."

This sounded logical. In any group there are several levels of people in control at the top. It was only natural that a vacancy would have been filled by somebody close to the fallen leader. The United States, as many other countries do, has such a system spelled out in its constitution. Article II assigns the Vice President as the successor, should the president be unable to "discharge the powers and duties of said office."

"Okay," I said. "Let's say I believe everything you're telling me. This all happened nearly thirty years ago. Why are we going to Cuba now?"

"New information from the Soviets," he explained as we turned off the road into a long gravel driveway blocked by an aged iron gate. "Since Gorbachev took over in April, our countries have been sharing a lot more intelligence with each other."

"The Soviets?" I asked. I thought we were talking about Nazis.

He held a finger to his lips to silence me and stopped in front of the gate. As he cranked down the window, I noticed a rusty intercom mounted on top of a cement post that appeared to be non-operational. I searched the tall fence on either side of the gate for some indication of where we were and found a faded sign near the ground that read, "La Comedia".

Sully pushed a small, dusty red button on the intercom and soon rapid Spanish was exchanged between him and an unknown male voice from the box. He rolled up the window as the heavy gate opened noisily in front of us, and I descended further into the mysterious world of the group known only as 'The Committee'.

Chapter 7

"What does 'La Comedia' mean?" I asked as we drove up the long gravel driveway toward a modest-sized house that appeared quite old and was sadly in need of repair. From a distance, it was difficult to tell for sure if it was just the slope of the ground or if the whole structure was actually leaning to one side.

He chuckled. "The comedy."

I frowned, not understanding. "The comedy?" I asked.

"It's sort of an inside joke. In other countries we always refer to ourselves as 'The Comedy' which is, of course, quite similar to 'The Committee' when spoken in English. But once translated, it's usually not close at all. It's a very effective method of code that we employ often. It started at our location in East Germany called 'die Komödie'—the German for 'committee' being 'Ausschuss'. In fact, for many years now, we have had a place in Moscow called 'Komediya', which is actually a working comedy club."

"Good cover," I commented, impressed with the simplicity of the code.

"We use rhymes as a code for many things, sort of like the rhyming slang popular in Britain." I was vaguely familiar with the concept. In college there had been a British student in my fraternity, and he would occasionally confuse us with some weird expression. Often the rhyming part of the phrase had been dropped to further conceal its meaning. One of my favorites was the use of the word "bacons" for "legs". We were walking across campus one summer afternoon, and he pointed to a cute girl saying, "She's sure got nice bacons." The rest of us just frowned at him in confusion. He explained that the saying came from "bacon and eggs", which of course rhymed with "legs".

"If someone is listening in," Sully continued, "by the time they translate it to their own language the rhymes no longer work. Of course, if the eavesdroppers speak fluent English then it's less effective, but most of the people we're worried about are using other languages."

"This house belongs to The Committee?" I asked. We had navigated the long driveway and were now parking outside the front entrance. The building looked even worse than I had initially thought, and I began to doubt the President's 'creative accounting' abilities—although I wasn't sure if that was a good or a bad thing. Large sections of shingles were missing, and it took some searching to find any signs of paint on the exterior walls. Most of the windows had been boarded up, and a large tree branch lay on the roof. "It looks like the place should be condemned," I observed, scrutinizing a gutter hanging off the east end of the house.

"Yes," he nodded, killing the engine, "another effective way of concealing its true purpose."

As we entered the house, I saw how correct he was. Although the inside was still clearly an old structure, it had been expertly supported from within. I counted at least ten different 8x8 wood posts angling in all different directions in the large great room, giving the sagging roof and walls the impression of a paraplegic balancing on crutches. I admired the engineering brilliance of it. They had found a way to prop up the failing exterior of the house while avoiding any outside indications that it was livable.

I surveyed the room and found that while the structure was hardly worth the materials it was made out of, the furnishings were quite the opposite. I saw two men reclining on antique looking leather sofas at opposite ends of the room. One was reading a thick book, and the other was watching some sort of footage from a security camera on a small TV. A large oak bookcase spanned the wall to my left, packed full of what appeared to be mostly reference books. On the opposite wall, a projection screen extended several feet down from the ceiling.

"Hey guys, here's the newbie," Sully announced, hanging the car keys on a hook inside the door. There were nine other sets of keys lined up on their respective hooks. It reminded me of a valet board. I hadn't seen any other cars outside and wondered what all the keys were for.

Sully's announcement got the men's attention, and they abandoned their work temporarily to offer various greetings. He motioned to the small red-haired man sitting closest to us who had paused the video he was watching.

"This is Brenton," Sully explained. Apparently last names did not exist. "We call him Mickey."

"Irish?" I asked.

"Nah, I'm from Utah," Mickey said from the couch. Then he pointed at his hair and spoke in a bad Irish accent. "But these guys think anyone with red hair is from Ireland."

"He's great with audio/video equipment," Sully said. "You need anything watched or listened to, come to him."

"Nice to meet you," Mickey nodded before returning to his work.

Sully proceeded across the room toward the next couch and I followed, ducking under a support beam on the way. "This is Tank," he said as we approached a large man with blond hair and blue eyes. Tank set his book on the couch and rose to shake my hand. Upon standing, he was even bigger than I initially thought. He had to be at least six and half feet tall, and from his broad weight lifter's shoulders, I thought he could probably make it as an NFL tight end.

"Welcome," Tank said gently, his low voice booming throughout the room. I reached for his outstretched hand and was astonished at how small mine looked in comparison. Thankfully, he didn't crush my fingers as I feared he might have, though I was quite sure he could.

"Tank?" I asked. "Another nickname?"

He smiled. "Nope, that's my legal name." Sully chuckled, and I sensed there was more to the story, but when they didn't offer, I figured it was better not to ask.

"And what is it that you do?" I asked Tank instead. I smiled wryly, because it was obvious that he was the strong arm of the group.

He smiled. "Believe it or not, I'm a physicist."

"Oh, physics," I nodded. "I'm sort of a physics buff myself. I considered minoring in it in college." Sully laughed at my naivety. I was assuming that Tank was the muscle man who was also interested in physics as a sort of hobby.

"No, I don't think you quite understand," he said. "He's not just a 'physics buff'. Tank has a PhD in theoretical physics from MIT."

"Wow," I said, sufficiently impressed. "I guess you really can't judge a book by its cover, can you?"

"Yeah, yeah. We're all real impressed with the giant's brain," said a voice behind me. "I was the first black man to graduate from my high school." I turned around to see a skinny, very dark-skinned man walk into the room from a hallway. He was so dark, it almost looked like someone had applied eye black to his entire face.

"Black?" I teased. "I thought you guys wanted to be called 'African American' now."

"Why would I want that?" he retorted. "I'm from Canada, and I've never even been to Africa." He smiled and glanced at Sully. "Well, not officially anyway."

"Canada?" I said in surprise.

"Yeah, why? You got a problem with that?"

"No," I corrected, "I was just under the impression that this group was all Americans."

"Name's Jackson," he introduced himself, shaking my hand, "and I'm both. Dad was from New York but worked in Ottawa. He married a Canadian woman and I was born with dual citizenship. I grew up in Kingston, across the border from up-state New York. After high school, I came to the U.S. for college."

I glanced around the room. "So, is it just the four of you then?" I asked. "Or are there more?"

"Five now," Sully corrected, nodding at me. "And this is just one group. There are others as well, but we don't know each other for the most part. Only the President knows everyone. As you're aware, this is a very covert organization, and even the different sections of The Committee don't know what the other parts are doing."

"Unless they screw up of course," Tank said with disgust.

"What do you mean?" I asked.

"How new are you?" Jackson exclaimed.

Sully laughed and shook his head. "He just met with George this morning for the first time."

"This morning?" Mickey whined. "How is he supposed to be any help to us?"

"He'll be fine," Sully replied sternly. "I chose him, remember?"

"So," I interjected, hoping to move the conversation off of me, "what were you saying about doing the wrong thing?"

Sully explained, "Did you ever read The Scarlet Letter?"

"Yeah, in high school," I said, thinking back a few years. "I don't remember much of it though. That's the one where the woman is caught sleeping around, right?"

"And her punishment is that she has to wear a big red A, for adultery," Jackson reminded me.

"Well," Sully continued, "if a member of The Committee ever turns against his team or his country, he is likewise marked with an 'A'."

"An 'A'? For what?" I was running through A-words in my head and was drawing a blank.

"Alligator," Mickey interjected from across the room.

I thought for a moment, then remembered the rhyming slang and nodded knowingly, "Traitor."

"Exactly," continued Sully. "If that happens, a picture of the offender is distributed to the other groups with a small red 'A' in the corner. He immediately has a network of highly intelligent and well-funded people across the globe hunting for him."

"Okay, I'll keep that in mind," I said. I could only imagine how many of these groups were out there, and what they would do with the 'marked man' when they found him. "And does this happen often?"

"Not really. Only a couple times ever that I know of."

"And we'd like to keep it that way," Tank added menacingly.

"You don't have to worry about me," I assured them. "I wouldn't know how to commit treason even if I wanted to."

"Good."

"So, what's this new intel from the Soviets I keep hearing about?" I asked as my curiosity took over. Sully looked to Mickey, who reached over to an open laptop computer, and hit a few keys. I was surprised to see full color images on the thin computer screen. We'd used desktop versions of a computer in college for some of our experiments, and I'd had a professor with one of these small, so-called 'laptop' computers, but his had only been a word processor. I didn't know components capable of handling images could be made small enough to fit in a portable case.

Apparently the computer was even linked to a projector somehow, because on the large screen hanging from the ceiling, I saw a grainy profile shot of a middle-aged man with a thick beard. It looked like it had been taken from a long distance and then enlarged after the photo was developed.

"I received this from a contact that I share info with from time to time," Mickey said, motioning to the picture. "We believe he is the bird of the Yahtzees." I looked at Sully in confusion.

"Leader of the Nazis," he said softly, not wanting to interrupt Mickey. "Rhyming slang, remember? Bird feeder, leader." I could tell this was going to take a little getting used to.

"Don't know what his name is yet, but according to the Bumbles, he took over in '62," Mickey continued. "I've been going over old footage from here in Strawberry and he's definitely involved with the Maestro."

"Okay," I interrupted, thoroughly lost, "I'm sorry, but I have no idea what you're talking about." It sounded like they were discussing Saturday morning cartoons. Bumbles? Strawberry? Maestro?

Mickey paused as Sully explained, "The Bumble bees are the KGB. Strawberry Banana is Havana, and the Maestro..."

"Is Castro," I finished. That was the easy one.

Sully nodded approvingly, "See, you're catching on."

"We've had him identified as a player for years," Mickey continued, "but never thought he would be at the bottle of the organization." He paused to allow me to work it out. A bottle of water? Father? No, that didn't make sense. Bottle cap? No. A bottle of pop maybe? Pop... hop? cop? top? That was it, top. I motioned for him to continue. "He's been making regular trips to Strawberry, and we thought he was some sort of messenger. Supposedly, the Bumbles have a guy on the inside."

"And we trust them?" I asked skeptically. "I mean, they haven't exactly been friendly with us for quite a few years."

"Doveryai, no proveryai," Tank said.

"Trust but verify," I translated, happy for the chance to show I knew something. I recognized the Russian phrase that President Reagan had been fond of using during his years in office.

"That's right," Tank said with surprise.

"I took some Russian in College," I explained. "So, how did you verify it?"

"We haven't," Mickey said bluntly. "That's what you're going to do."

"Me?" I didn't understand. "What can I do?"

Sully shrugged. "Well, really any of us could do it, but since you're the newbie, you get to go in."

"Go in?" I said, feeling tricked. "No, I was just supposed to get some intel. I don't go on missions, or field trips, or whatever you want to call them."

"Baptism by fire," Jackson laughed.

"I think I was already baptized on the plane," I offered, thinking back to the wet shirt I had worn all afternoon.

"Relax," Sully said. "Jackson's going with you." This didn't make me feel much better. If I had to pick one of them to tag along, it would have been Tank, but he did stand out somewhat in Cuba with his blond hair and excessive stature. Jackson, on the other hand, blended in nicely with the ten percent of the population that was of African descent. As they explained the plan to me, my fears were assuaged only a little. It seemed like it would be simple enough, but I'd never done anything like it before.

Chapter 8

I was surprised by how easily we entered the home of Fidel Castro on the western end of Havana. Mickey had been doing surveillance for about a week and knew the family would be out of town for a couple days. Therefore, it was assumed that security would be light.

Apparently the Comandante relied on the secrecy of the location for much of his protection. A wall of large pine trees surrounded the property, making it nearly impossible to see from the outside. In addition, all streets surrounding the house were one way streets leading away, effectively preventing anyone from happening upon the entrance accidentally.

Although the house was large by Cuban standards, I was surprised at how nonextravagent it was. There was little in the way of landscaping, save for a few shrubs along the house, and the patchy grass was sorely in need of mowing. The darkness of night made it difficult to see well, but it appeared some of the brown paint was even peeling off the exterior walls. I knew people back home that took better care of their barns.

As we hid in the trees, I wondered aloud if we were in the wrong place, but then I saw a man in military fatigues traversing the front yard with a Kalashnikov hanging from a sling over his shoulder. Jackson just laughed.

"Nevermind," I corrected myself. "This is the place."

Satisfied with the level of protection, Jackson climbed back into the driver's seat of the white panel van we had arrived in, and I hurried in next to him. We bounced the wrong way down a pot hole-ridden street and up the gravel driveway toward the house. The guard spun around quickly as he heard the van approaching and stepped out into the driveway, waving for us to stop.

I said a quick prayer as the guard approached the vehicle, gun in hand, and Jackson cranked open the window. My heart was beating so loudly, I worried that the man might be able to hear it from outside the van. *Just keep it together*, I told myself. *If you act like you're supposed to be here, he'll believe it.*

"Quién es usted?" the guard demanded, pointing at Jackson with the rifle in his hands. I had a momentary panic attack as I saw the gun up close. I tried to steady my breathing and stared through the windshield at the house, pretending to be bored. As he had practiced earlier, Jackson told the man in Spanish that we were delivering a new TV that Castro ordered to replace the broken one inside. Mickey had explained that while the Comandante liked to project an air of equality with his countrymen—hence the rundown-looking house—he did allow himself the luxury of a nice television to watch foreign news reports. We were counting on the guard not having firsthand knowledge of the condition of the current TV.

The man nodded, appearing not the least bit alarmed, and waved us by, stepping back into the grass. He seemed bored, and I figured he was probably second-string if he was guarding an empty building. We parked near the front door and removed the big screen from the back of the van. As we juggled the heavy box, the guard set his gun on the ground and leaned it against a dead shrub. He began walking our way, apparently planning to help, but Jackson quickly explained that it was company policy that we install it ourselves; that way if anything went wrong there would be no arguments over who was at fault. After a momentary hesitation, the guard shrugged and returned to his patrol, disappearing around the north side of the house.

Once inside, I was happy to learn that Mickey had indeed done his homework, as the TV currently in Castro's living room looked very similar to the one we had just carried in. It didn't have to be perfect, just close enough for a casual observer, like the one stomping around the yard outside. Obviously, we did not want Fidel coming home to find a new TV and asking questions, so after we were done, we would simply take the new one back out to the van, and the guard would assume we had switched them.

With precious little time before inviting suspicion, I searched the house while Jackson kept an eye on the sentry through a kitchen window. In the moonlight, the guard was easily visible as he wandered through a line of evergreens at the edge of the property, looking at the stars more than any potential threats.

I started in the den, which was sparsely appointed with a modest desk in the center of the room, a small bookshelf along one wall, and a writing table on another. Looming over the desk from the back wall hung a faded portrait of a much younger Fidel Castro. I peeked briefly behind the painting and the bookshelf, but found no secret hiding places.

Moving to the desk, I rifled through papers and snapped pictures as quickly as I could. Since my Spanish was weak and we couldn't remove anything, the plan was to take pictures of each page and translate them back at La Comedia. I was surprised by how little was in the small desk. I had always envisioned

Castro's residence as being filled with fancy antique furniture, as most dictators had, but this was the exact opposite. I was pretty sure that my meager apartment back home was fancier than his place. I took that as a sign of how bad Cuba's economy really was. If this was how the best of the best lived, what were things like for the poor?

From the den, I moved to the living room, checking a small bookcase in the corner and the end table by the couch. Then, just when I was about to let Jackson know I was done, a thought flashed through my mind and I jogged down the narrow hallway to the master bedroom. I was a nocturnal creature myself and often worked in bed late into the night. Something told me this man might be the same.

Entering the bedroom, I surveyed the furniture—a tall dresser sat along the wall just inside the door, while a longer vanity-type dresser with a mirror adorned the opposite side of the room. In the center was a king-sized bed and a night stand on either side. I noticed a cigar box resting on the corner of the taller dresser, and it occurred to me that since I was in Cuba, I could legally buy Cuban cigars, unlike back home. Perhaps my counterfeit Mexican passport would come in handy after all.

I briefly checked the top drawer of the dresser but found nothing of interest, so I moved on to the nightstands. There was some sort of Spanish romance novel on the far table. I couldn't read the title, but the picture was pretty clear. Fidel didn't strike me as that kind of a reader, so I decided that side most likely belonged to his wife. The other was my target.

The bedside table had a large drawer—about the size one might find on a file cabinet—below a solitary shelf six inches from the top. I removed three small books, also with Spanish titles that I didn't recognize, and found the usual nightstand adornments inside, but no work related materials. I shut the drawer and returned the books with a sigh, then stood and turned to leave. Halfway to the hall door I stopped suddenly.

I had that familiar feeling that I got whenever something wasn't right, but I couldn't place it. A flag had just been thrown on the field, but the referee's mic wasn't working, and I couldn't decipher what was wrong. I never understood how my brain could know something was amiss, yet I didn't know. Sometimes it felt like I had two brains, and they kept secrets from each other. *Toss the potato already!* I wanted to say.

I pulled the books from the small table again, but upon closer inspection, they still looked perfectly normal, aside from being in Spanish. I slowly shook my head; what was it that my subconscious had noticed? I dropped the books back onto the shelf for the second time and suddenly grasped what was wrong. The sound wasn't right. Despite the poor quality of craftsmanship and the thin wood the table was made out of, the books generated more of a thud, as if hitting something solid. I carefully slid the nightstand away from the wall and saw it had no back.

Bending over to look inside, I discovered what had caused the noise.

About two inches below the shelf, a second one had been added which was not visible from the front, and the back of the large drawer had been cut out to allow it to open without catching on the concealed compartment. Sitting on the hidden shelf was another cigar box, barely able to squeeze between the two pieces of wood. The box must have dampened the vibrations of the shelf above it when I set the books down, making it sound more solid than it really was.

I considered that there was a box of cigars in plain sight on the nearby dresser and felt fairly confident that Fidel was not hiding his smoking from his wife. Certainly something important was in there. Carefully sliding the box out, I noted the direction it was facing, and laid it on the bed. I paused and glanced around the room, suddenly paranoid that I might get caught. I could hear Jackson tapping on the counter in the kitchen, probably bored. Reassuring myself that I was still alone, I lifted the lid and felt my heart skip a beat when I saw hand-written letters that appeared to be addressed to Castro himself.

I spread the pages carefully onto the bed, forming a grid pattern. I needed to keep the pages in order so they would be easy to return to their hiding place. We didn't want to give Fidel any reason to be suspicious. Working from the bottom of the stack, I laid each page next to the previous one with the edges overlapping slightly, sort of like shingling a house. Before long I had twenty-four letters arranged in four rows of six.

I began to snap pictures of the pages individually and discovered it was a more difficult task than I had initially thought. In order to frame the picture correctly, the camera had to be held out over the bed. However, when I did this, I could no longer see through the view finder. I soon found myself in the awkward position of standing on the edge of the bed, balancing myself with one hand on the ceiling fan above, and taking photographs with the other.

I was starting to get into a groove and had half of the pages done, when I heard Jackson whistling from the other room. It sounded like the beginning to "Oh, Canada", but I didn't have time to find out. The whistle was the sign that the guard was coming, and I knew I was running out of time. Quickly, I snapped wide shots of four pages at a time, hoping that the writing would still be legible. Although in a hurry, I tried to remain calm and hold the camera steady to ensure the images would be in focus.

I congratulated myself for my foresight as I stacked the pages back up. Since I had overlapped the papers on the bed, each row slid easily into a nice pile. I dropped the stack of letters in the box and quickly returned it to its hiding place. As I slid the nightstand back toward the wall, I was careful to align the legs on the indentations in the carpet where it had previously sat.

Satisfied that my presence would not be detected, I turned to face the bedroom door when I heard the front door open. I was momentarily frozen in terror, as I pictured the AK in my mind. I glanced around the room, hastily searching for an escape route, then a thought abruptly jumped into my head, and I darted across the hall and into the bathroom. I took a few deep breaths, trying to calm my quickening pulse, and flushed the toilet.

Knowing a man with a large gun waited for me, I forced my feet to return me to the living room, where I found the guard eyeing Jackson suspiciously. As I entered the room, he pointed down the hallway with the rifle. "Donde esta?" he demanded.

"Yo necesitaba un baño," I explained, grabbing my stomach and grimacing to indicate I was having bowel issues. "La comida de mi suegra," I added with a shrug, blaming the problems on my mother-in-law's cooking. I hoped that I had remembered the translation correctly. It was something my high school Spanish teacher had often said about his own mother-in-law, except he had been talking about how great her food was. The guard seemed satisfied by my explanation and slowly lowered the rifle back down to his side.

He nodded to the TV sitting in the middle of the room. "Terminaste?" he half asked, half ordered. Jackson acknowledged that yes, we were done, and we hurriedly carried the "broken" television back out to the van.

We bid the guard "adios" with a smile and polite wave and sped back to La Comedia to examine the photos.

Chapter 9

hile waiting for Mickey to develop the negatives in a back room, I perused the massive wall of books. They appeared to be sorted by subject and covered everything one would ever need to know. I found books on the sciences, explosives, linguistics, military strategy, construction how-to's, cook books, and the historical accounts of several countries.

"You guys have everything here," I commented over my shoulder at Sully and Jackson, who were engaged in a game of chess nearby. Jackson seemed to be accumulating a good number of his opponent's pieces, but Sully remained calm, always appearing to be in control.

"Just about," Jackson responded, placing Sully in check.

"And it looks to be sorted by subject?"

"Yeah, the best we can anyway. It makes it easier when you are researching something." I reached the far end of the room and chuckled to myself as I noticed something odd.

"What?" Sully asked, finally moving out of check.

"Nothing," I said. "I just thought it was interesting that you have the Bible and 'On the Order of the Species' grouped together." This seemed to get their attention, and they looked up from their game.

"And is that because you feel that the Bible isn't science," Jackson asked, "or because Darwin isn't religion?"

"It's not that I don't think they go together. I'm just surprised that you guys think they do." I had always heard that scientific consensus was for evolution, and I would have thought a group of scientists would feel the same. I was actually surprised to see the Bible at all.

"What doesn't go together?" Mickey asked, emerging from the back room.

"Oh great. Here we go," Jackson groaned.

"I was just commenting on the fact that you have the Bible and Darwin grouped together on the shelves," I explained.

Mickey opened his mouth to respond, but was interrupted by Jackson. "We're not getting into this

THE NAZI CONSPIRACY

again." Mickey shot him a fiery glare, and I got the impression that there had been some heated debate in the past.

Mickey seemed all too eager to resume the discussion. "It's not my fault that some people here prefer to believe a fairy tale over actual facts."

Tank now abandoned his snack and called from the kitchen, "Fairy tale? So, you reject the possibility of God, something that 95% of Americans believe in?"

"Hey, I just go where the evidence leads me," Mickey replied defensively. "And you have to admit, most of that 95% aren't rational thinkers."

"Come on, guys," Sully interjected. "We've got work to do. You can debate this later."

"Why do they have to be mutually exclusive?" I asked. The others turned to me, evidently surprised by my contribution to the dispute.

"Well, the bible says that God created the Earth and everything in it, including man, and that it only happened a few thousand years ago," Tank said, as if the answer was obvious. I knew where the disagreement came from, but chose to act ignorant at the moment. I'd had this discussion several times in religion classes in college and had learned how to form my argument.

"Right," I nodded. "I get that. That's not a problem."

"Yeah, yeah," Jackson said with a dismissive wave of his hand. "We've heard it before. Maybe the

75

days in Genesis were really long and evolution happened, guided by God. It's possible, but most creationists don't like that one."

"No, that's not what I meant," I pressed, then I turned to Tank. "How old was Adam when God created him?"

He considered the question for a moment. "I don't know exactly... maybe a teenager? He could've been in his 30s or 40s. The Bible doesn't specify."

"But he wasn't a baby?"

He shrugged. "I would say... probably not. There would have been no one to take care of him. And besides, he talked to God, so he was probably grown already."

"Exactly!" I declared. "He was already grown. And Eve, she was grown too, correct?"

"Yes. God gave him a wife, not a child."

"And the animals, same thing," I continued. "Plants? Probably grown too. The animals would need something to eat, and a bunch of seeds in the ground wouldn't do them much good."

"What's your point?" Mickey demanded impatiently.

"My point is that when," I paused and glanced at Mickey, "sorry, *if* God created people, they appeared as though they had been babies and advanced through the normal stages of life. He created them with a past, in a sense."

Sully was smiling at me, and I could see he knew where I was headed. "So, why couldn't He have created the Earth as if it were already in the middle of its life, as if it had a past?"

I nodded approvingly. "Exactly." Tank and Mickey both sat in silence, searching for a way to protest.

"So," Mickey said finally, "God created an Earth that had already evolved?"

"Sure. Why not?" I asked. "I don't see anything that conflicts with it in Genesis." I looked to Tank questioningly, but he was lost in thought.

"Seems like kind of a clever side step to me," Mickey retorted. "You can't just explain everything by saying 'God did it'."

"I like it," Tank declared with a nod. I wasn't sure if that was because it made sense, or because Mickey was against it. "I'll have to give it some thought," he added, "but it's very creative."

"Good," Jackson said, clapping his hands together to signify the end of the conversation. "Then let's get to work."

Having the best handle on the Spanish language, Sully took charge of translating the documents. Mickey placed the developed negatives on a small, magnifying overhead projector. The colors were all reversed, appearing black with white text on the negative, but they were still readable, and no one wanted to wait for actual photos to develop.

"Start with the last fifteen pictures," I directed, drawing surprised looks from everyone.

"Why? What did you find?" Mickey asked.

77

I shrugged. "Just a hunch." As Mickey slid the strip of film along the screen, I explained how I had discovered the pages in the mysterious cigar box. "I just hope they're not love letters from an old girlfriend," I joked.

"Wouldn't surprise me," Jackson remarked. "What's the count up to now, three of his kids born out of wedlock?"

"That we know of," Tank added.

Sully was silently skimming the first page, and from the slight smile that formed on his face, I knew we had found something. "This is a letter addressed to the Maestro," he said excitedly, "and it's from the Juror himself! This is unbelievable."

I frowned. "From the Juror?"

"Yeah, you know Hitler, the Führer. Juror?" Sully said over his shoulder, never removing his eyes from the text.

I shook my head. "No, I figured that one out. I'm just disappointed," I explained. "That would mean these letters are nearly thirty years old and will give us little insight into the current makeup of the group."

"Let's see the other ones," Sully said, ignoring my pessimism, and Mickey complied. The next few were also from the 'Juror', and I felt all of my excitement being sucked out. Then on page six, the handwriting suddenly changed. I skipped to the bottom and read the salutation aloud, "Tu amigo, Evan Brown."

"Who's Evan Brown?" Jackson asked. "Do we know him?"

"No," Sully asserted. I doubted that he knew the names and aliases of every person they had gathered information on, but decided not to question his confidence. "This is our guy," he declared, reading through the letter.

"What does it say?" I asked.

"It's basically just letting the Maestro know that the writer, Evan, is taking over for the Juror," Sully explained. "It also mentions the possibility of retaliation against Potus." Potus, an acronym for 'President of the United States' used by the Secret Service, was a term I was familiar with. Maybe the nut jobs were right, and Oswald really had been hired by the Cubans, or even the Nazis.

As Mickey continued through the pages, it appeared they were in chronological order. This made sense, because I had kept them in order when I removed them from the cigar box and had taken the pictures backwards—from the bottom of the stack to the top. About halfway through, we got to an image of four pages, instead of one.

"What'd you do, Mickey?" Sully complained, moving closer to squint at the screen.

"Nothing," he snapped back. "That's what the picture looks like."

Sully glanced at me questioningly, and I explained that I had run out of time and didn't want to miss any pages. He nodded, approving my decision, although he was clearly disappointed. It was harder to read them now, but Mickey made some adjustments and was able to zoom in on the notes enough to decipher the writing. We continued reading, and eventually got to some more recent letters. I listened intently as Sully translated:

12 November 1989

President Castro,

Recent events have caused us to pursue a different approach. President Botha's resignation in August was a strong blow to our cause, and Mandela's all but certain release from prison in the coming months will end our hold on the country. We are shifting our focus to another, more volatile region we've been working in, where the influence of Moscow and Washington will be less effective. This is to be given the highest confidentiality; I cannot stress that enough. We will require the assistance of several of your top military personnel, whomever you can spare. I will send instructions soon. Please have your men ready to depart quickly. I will be in contact within the next month with details.

Your brother in arms,
Evan Brown

"Did you say Mandela?" I asked, thinking I must have heard him wrong.

"Yup," Sully said. "President Botha of South Africa was just forced into retirement last year. Apparently that's why Gorbachev was so intent on ending apartheid."

"The Juror was in South Africa?" Tank said, almost to himself, as he processed the revelation.

"So, I take it you didn't know that South Africa was being controlled by the Na... I mean Yahtzees?" I asked.

Sully shook his head. "No, but Reagan was curious why Gorbachev was pushing so hard to change things back in '88. They met in Moscow to discuss the situation and threatened President Botha with military action if he didn't relinquish control of Namibia. That meeting was directly related to Botha's forced retirement and Mandela's release this year." I felt completely out of the loop and realized how ignorant I was about international affairs. I had heard of Mandela of course and vaguely remembered that he had recently been released from prison, but I didn't know any of the details.

"I knew it," Tank exclaimed. "I told you guys they would be working in Africa."

"Yeah, yeah, but you didn't know it was *South Africa*," Mickey argued.

"That's just semantics," Tank shot back.

"It doesn't matter," Sully interrupted. "Where are they now is the question."

"What is more volatile than South Africa?" I asked, motioning to the letter on the screen.

"Libya?" Tank guessed. "Or whatever it is they're calling it now..."

"The Great Socialist People's Libyan Arab Jamahiriya," Sully said, as if answering a trivia question. Obviously the books on the wall were not just for show.

"You just can't get off Africa, can you?" Mickey mocked.

"Well, Gaddafi's not exactly friendly with the U.S.," Tank argued, but his speculation was shot down by the group as they noted that Libya was loosely aligned with the Soviets, and that the United States had even had several hostile interactions with the country in recent years. It wasn't exactly what one would consider to be a country where "the influence of Moscow and Washington will be less effective."

"How 'bout Germany?" Jackson offered. "The Berlin wall just came down."

"True," Sully agreed, "but I think that would make it less volatile, not more. Besides, I doubt the Yahtzees are gonna be back there any time soon. Didn't work out so well last time."

"Well, you guys are the experts," I said, "but my first thought was the Middle East." It seemed like Israel would never get along with its neighbors.

"No way!" Mickey exclaimed suddenly, staring at the screen.

"What?" Sully asked.

"It's gotta be a coincidence..." Mickey said to himself, ignoring the question.

"Mickey, what is it?" Sully demanded.

Mickey glanced sideways at us and then pointed at the screen. "Doesn't that name seem a little familiar?" I looked at the screen again. The letters were all signed by Evan Brown, but it didn't ring any bells. I searched my brain for a memory of the name but came up with nothing.

"Eva Braun," Jackson declared finally. Of course! Eva Braun was Hitler's wife who had supposedly committed suicide with him.

"Do you think Evan Brown could be the son of Adolf and Eva Hitler?" I asked. The room was silent as everyone processed the question. I felt a chill come over me as I considered the possibility of a family of Hitlers.

"That would make sense," Sully finally offered. "They were living in secret for twenty years. Why wouldn't they have had kids? I don't know why we never considered it before."

"And it seems only natural that Adolf would be succeeded by a son," Mickey added. He spun around quickly and hit a few keys on his laptop. The image he had received from his KGB contact appeared again on the screen. We all crowded around, studying the picture more intently this time. I squinted and tried to imagine the man with a toothbrush mustache and a Nazi military uniform.

"I don't know," Tank said, shaking his head. "It doesn't really look like Adolf."

"Maybe he takes after his mother," I offered.

"There's one more letter," Jackson pointed out. "Why don't we see what it has to say?"

Sully returned to the screen and continued translating.

Chapter 10

I awoke with a start, not knowing where I was. All around me I heard a deafening roar, reminiscent of the wind tunnel I had used a couple times in college. As I opened my eyes, I sat up and tried to focus. I appeared to be in some sort of large dark room with an arched ceiling. And what was that noise? The racket was such that I couldn't concentrate on anything else. How did I get here? I thought back, but couldn't remember lying down to go to sleep. Had I dozed off at work again? No, this was definitely not my lab. Where was I?

I shook my head to remove the cobwebs and glanced to my right, where I saw Mickey sleeping in the seat next to me. Suddenly it all came back—Sully,

the fake passport, the Committee, and breaking into
Fidel's house. After deciphering the code in the notes,
the five of us had crammed ourselves into the small
Grand Prix and hurriedly left La Comedia. We did
not return to Havana, however, and instead drove
further out into the country to the east, stopping near
a large open field. Waiting for us in the meadow was
a United States Air Force C-141 cargo plane. It was an
impressive aircraft, and although it was somewhat
smaller than the 747 I had flown to Cuba on, it looked
enormous sitting out in the middle of nowhere with
only small trees around.

Two men were lounging near the plane until
we arrived, and they quickly jumped to attention,
putting out their cigarettes as we pried ourselves out of
the car. Sully conversed briefly with our pilots as the
rest of us climbed on board.

Inside, the plane seemed even larger. As a
cargo plane, the bulk of the fuselage was empty space,
and from within, it felt like the biggest airliner I had
ever been on. There were seats facing inward along
the outside walls, and we quickly strapped ourselves
in. Within a matter of minutes, the powerful engines
were roaring and we left Cuba under cover of
darkness. Somewhere over the Atlantic I had drifted
off.

I wondered how far we had gone while I was
out. Were we even over the ocean still? I tipped my
head to the side and attempted to stretch out the knot
that had formed in my neck while I slept. My eyes

adjusted slowly, and I surveyed the rest of the cargo hold we were riding in. I saw that along with Mickey, Jackson and Tank were also sleeping further toward the back of the plane. Sitting across from me, Sully studied a map, apparently trying to plan out the way to our destination. Something had been bothering me ever since we boarded the plane back in Cuba, and I decided to confer with him about it now.

"So, where are we gonna land?" I shouted over the noise of the engines.

"What do you mean?" he asked, looking up from his map.

"Well, it's not like we're exactly going into friendly territory. We can't just..."

"No, I get that," he interrupted. "But what do you mean 'land'?"

That was exactly what I was afraid of. I shook my head emphatically. "No, no. I can't parachute."

"Sure you can," he replied with a dismissive wave. "It's easy."

"No, you don't understand," I explained. "I have a thing with heights."

When I was nine—and after much coaxing on my part—my dad had decided to build me a tree house. I knew I would be the envy of every kid on the block, and I was very excited. Once he had the floor done, he took me up to see it. I felt like I was on top of the world; I could see all the way over the roof of the McHenrys' house next door.

SCOTT STROSAHL

I had been nervous about the distance from the ground and stayed close to my dad at the center of the platform. But even more so, I was excited for it to be finished. I was sure I had never been happier in my few years on earth, when abruptly a bird from a nearby branch flew past me, right in front of my face. I was startled and stumbled backward toward the edge, grasping for anything my little fingers could get a hold of...

"You'll be fine," Sully said, waving his hand dismissively. "I'll talk you through it." I wasn't so sure, but there wasn't much I could do about it at that point. I couldn't just stay on the plane. Who knew where it would end up? "Just remember," he added with a smile, "getting to the ground is the easy part."

"And what happens when I have a heart attack on the way down?" I retorted.

He shrugged. "Well, then we probably bury you in the mountains, and your girlfriend gets a hundred grand and no explanation." I thought of Katie and wondered how upset she was that I had missed our dinner.

"There's nothing you can do about it now. Just focus on the mission at hand and don't worry about it." I decided to take his advice and set my mind on where we were going.

The words from the last letter still echoed in my head—"Today we resurrect our quest to rid this lost world of everything inferior." It had taken some time to decipher what came next:

88

I trust you received my letter of two weeks ago. Hopefully preparations have gone well, and you are ready to provide us with the assistance we will need. Per the usual method, the location is provided below.

Your friend,
Evan Brown

p.s. Lucky numbers: 11, 19, 4, 269

It was obvious that the "lucky numbers" were supposed to reveal the location, but decoding this cipher proved a bit more difficult. At first we tried latitude and longitude, but that failed mightily since 269 is too large to be either a degree or minute measurement. We tried letters of the Spanish alphabet, K-Q-D-?, but of course 269 again caused us some trouble.

After much discussion about the mathematical significance of the numbers—11, 19, and 269 are all primes—Tank again got stuck on Africa, more specifically Egypt. Apparently in the year AD 19, the Egyptians were exiled from Rome, and then in AD 269, Zenobia declared herself Queen of Egypt, partially burning the library at Alexandria. He couldn't come up with anything for the years 4 or 11, however, and the idea was quickly dismissed.

We decided that we needed to think simpler. Surely Castro wasn't expected to figure out complex mathematical formulas or know the history of the entire world. Eventually, it was suggested by Mickey that perhaps the numbers referred to the locations of words in the letter. However, there were not 269 words in any of the letters.

Working off of this theme, we tried counting the characters instead of words and found a surprising result. The final note had less than 269 characters, but when using the second to last page, dated November 12th, and counting the letters in the Spanish text, the numbers "11, 19, 4, 269" referred to the letters I-R-A-Q. And that was how I had found myself preparing to drop out of the sky over the Middle East.

"So, what's the plan then?" I asked. Sully held up the map for me to see. It was a map of the Middle East, including Iraq, Iran, and Saudi Arabia among other countries. He pointed at the eastern border of Iraq which was shared with Iran. I could see that the star marking Baghdad, the capital of Iraq, was not far from this border. He ran a finger along the Zagros Mountains, lining the inside border of Iran from north to south, and explained that we would fly in low over the mountains and jump from there. Once safely on the ground, we would cross the border into Iraq and make our way to Baghdad.

By flying low in the dark over Iran, we would minimize our chances of being detected by the Iraqis. Although I was still apprehensive about the jump, the plan seemed simple enough. I knew nothing about what type of radar capabilities the Iraqis or Iranians had, but something told me Sully probably knew the exact model numbers of their systems.

"Alright, we'd better start getting ready," Sully announced loudly, waking up the others.

"Already?" I could feel myself beginning to panic. For some reason I had thought I would have more time to prepare. The others stood and stretched lazily, seemingly not the least bit concerned, as Sully handed out parachutes. He helped me put mine on, showing me where each of the straps went. I tightened them until they almost hurt. It was quite uncomfortable, but I didn't care. It couldn't be any worse than colliding with the ground at full speed.

It felt like I was dreaming again as the large cargo bay door slowly opened, further increasing the engine noise. We were skipping across the tops of the mountains now, as we prepared to exit the plane by hurtling ourselves through the air at over a hundred miles per hour. My body stood up and slowly shuffled toward the increasingly large opening, but I was not controlling it. My mind was still sitting safely strapped in a seat, watching the events unfold.

"First time?" Jackson shouted in my ear, bringing me back to consciousness.

"Yeah," I nodded. "Is it that obvious?" He just shrugged.

"I'm not real great with heights," I explained. I was too frightened to be embarrassed.

"You'll be fine. It's easy. All you gotta do is jump and let gravity do the work. Just don't forget to pull the cord before you hit the ground." He laughed and slapped me on the back.

"Yeah, thanks a lot. That makes me feel much better."

"Alright, here's the deal," Sully interrupted, shouting at me from about a foot away. "We're flying in low, so we'll be deploying our chutes as soon as we are in the air. See this cable running from your pack to the ceiling? That will release your parachute as you leave the aircraft; you don't need to worry about pulling the cord. There will be a handle on either side of you that you use to steer. Try to stay somewhat close to us. We'll regroup after we land. Got it?" I nodded my understanding because I figured the growing knot in my throat would probably prohibit any audible speech.

Between the roar of the plane's mammoth engines, the hissing wind from the open door, and the unsteady floor I was standing on as the aircraft dipped and rose, I had no desire to stay on the plane much longer. However, I didn't feel a strong urge to plummet to my death over the mountains of Iran either. I willed my legs to plod further toward the back of the plane as my two brains played tug-of-war in my head. The wind became stronger as I approached the precipice, and I wondered how I would convince myself to actually jump.

Fortunately, I didn't have to.

Chapter 11

I stepped gingerly out onto the large cargo bay door that had been lowered to afford us an easy exit out the rear of the plane. Balancing on what was now the springboard for our insane plan, I leaned toward Sully and tried to shout some sort of excuse why I needed to stay in the plane. He just smiled and motioned toward the opening. I turned and saw Tank flash a toothy grin before doing a front flip out of the back of the plane. Jackson followed quickly behind with a diving barrel roll. *They are kids playing at the neighborhood pool*, I thought. I frowned as I noticed that neither of them had the cable attached to their backs that Sully had shown me earlier.

SCOTT STROSAHL

Then time slowed down. As I watched Tank
and Jackson tumbling into space, I felt something
collide with my back, and my body lurched violently
forward toward emptiness. Suddenly, I was nine
years old again and falling slowly toward the ground.
Above me, I could see the platform that was my
unfinished tree house. My dad lunged at me, reaching
for my outstretched hand. I watched as he shrank into
the distance, his eyes widening as he grasped only air
and I moved farther away. I started to yell for him,
but no sound came out. A branch zoomed past my
head, and I closed my eyes, bracing for the impact
with the ground. Then I felt a violent pull as
something abruptly yanked me back up away from the
ground.

The jerk from the parachute brought me back
to the present, and I looked around, dazed by what had
just happened. I was no longer on the plane; that
much was certain. Did I jump? Had Sully pushed
me? I turned to look behind me and saw him floating
under his own parachute, surprisingly close to me. He
just winked and smiled.

I looked down to my left and saw two more
parachutes below, presumably Tank and Jackson. My
stomach did a flip as I realized how quickly the
ground was getting closer. I panicked and grabbed for
anything I could reach, pulling on a handle suspended
above my right shoulder. The chute immediately
tipped and lurched sideways. I released the handle and
righted myself.

"Deep breaths," I said aloud. "People do this all the time. The parachute opened, so you're not gonna die. It'll be okay." I shook my head, trying to shock my brain back to life, and set my mind on staying close to someone. It didn't really matter who. The only thing I could imagine that was worse than jumping out of a perfectly good airplane, was being an American alone in the mountains of Iran.

It took a bit of experimenting to get the hang of steering, but once I figured it out, I kept my eyes on Sully and matched his moves, trying to keep him a uniform distance away. It was just like pacing a car on the highway, I told myself. As we neared the ground, or rather the trees, I guessed that Sully wasn't more than a hundred yards away, and I began to prepare for the impending collision with the Earth.

I wasn't really sure how to go about landing, but I'd seen videos of people doing it before and thought I was supposed to run as I hit the ground. Sully was pointing as he steered toward an open area where we could avoid being impaled by a tree, and then I saw it—a small river winding down the mountain. Water was usually softer than dirt, wasn't it? I hesitated a moment, unsure of what to do, then abandoned the clearing and steered sharply to my left, hoping there was still time to make it. I swooped low over a tall tree, taking out a few leaves with my shoes, and crashed into the cold water below.

To my delight, I found it was several feet deep and easily cushioned my fall. I stood and assessed the damages. I appeared to be in one piece, with no permanent scars from my first skydive. I soon realized, however, that a river landing might not have been as great of an idea as it had seemed from the air. Though the current was fairly strong, I could easily swim to shore without drifting too far; I was a strong swimmer and only about ten feet from dry land.

But when my parachute descended to the surface behind me, I promptly found myself being pulled downstream, and underwater, by the straps hooked to my vest. That large area of fabric that created the much needed drag in the air, created even more drag in the water. I struggled to release the cables, but I hadn't paid enough attention during that part of the two minute lesson on the plane. I had assumed that once we were on the ground, the others could help me. Of course, that only worked if I landed near the others.

Gasping for air, and gulping mostly water, a large tree branch came into view hanging low over the water just above me. I lunged for it before it could pass and felt my hand hit bark. I swung my other hand around the other side and pulled with all my might to lift my head out of the water. Readjusting my grip, I was able to connect my hands on the other side. I could feel the chute still tugging at my back, trying to drag me to certain death downstream. It felt like I was the rope in a game of tug of war.

I considered my options for a moment and was drawing a blank, when I saw a hand reaching down from the log above me. I followed the arm up to see Sully lying on his stomach. After landing, he must have come looking for me and shimmied out onto the tree branch. He quickly released the straps for the parachute, and almost immediately a large weight left my shoulders, both literally and figuratively.

"Thanks," I managed, as I pulled myself to shore with the branch.

"You of little faith. Still don't trust me, huh?" he joked as he walked above me, using the branch as a balance beam. I recalled moments earlier when he had pointed toward the clearing, and in my infinite wisdom I had chosen to ignore him and go the other way. Why did I doubt his expertise?

"Sorry," was all I could say as I wished for the first time that I could be back in my lab.

"Come on, let's go," he said, jogging along the shore upstream. I quickly caught up, not wanting to make the same mistake again. It was only a short distance to reach the clearing where the others were waiting. I found that their gear was already loaded into the back of a beat up blue and rust colored minivan that had apparently materialized out of the woods.

"Where did that come from?" I asked between breaths. Sully just flashed his mysterious smile, which I was becoming quite familiar with, and climbed in the open side door. I followed him in and slid the door shut.

Sitting in the open captain's chair in the middle row, I saw Tank and Mickey were in the front and Jackson lounged on the bench seat in the back. I considered pressing Sully for a response, but knew I probably wouldn't get a straight answer. And besides, I never would have known if he was telling the truth anyway. For all I knew, one of them had unfolded the van out of his pocket after we landed.

I looked out the window at the dark sky. The plane was nowhere in sight—here one minute, gone the next, with no evidence of our presence in a foreign country. Except, of course, for a large green parachute now floating downstream. Tank shifted the mystery van into gear, and we bounced across the clearing to a small dirt path through the woods.

Chapter 12

We drove quietly into Baghdad just before noon and, as expected, the city was bustling with people heading every which way. I felt self-conscious, like we were carrying signs that said 'American' on them, but no one paid any attention to another old van driving around the streets. We entered the city from the east, passing what appeared to be a military airport, and soon found ourselves on a large roundabout. I had experienced one of these stoplight alternatives a few times since moving to Pennsylvania, but they still seemed quirky to me since we had no such thing back home in Iowa.

Anxiously looking ahead toward our destination, I was surprised by the number of tall buildings on the skyline. For some reason, in my mind I had always pictured Baghdad as a cluster of old rundown buildings in the desert. Instead, I was greeted by a large municipality that Jackson informed me was home to more than four million citizens. That was slightly larger than the giant city of Los Angeles.

Traffic was light, and we were quickly following Al Rashid Street along the eastern bank of the Tigris. As I watched the water flow down the ancient river, I felt very small and insignificant. This waterway had been one of four that branched off of the river flowing through the Garden of Eden six thousand years earlier. I wondered how many billions of gallons of water had traveled down roughly this same path in the subsequent millennia.

It seemed like we had nearly crossed the entire city when Tank finally pulled the van off of the main road onto a side street and parked in front of a small building that I guessed was a convenience store. "It's Friday. We'll have to walk it," he announced. Everyone dutifully piled out and retrieved a bag from the back.

"What happens on Fridays?" I asked.

"The book market," Sully explained, and then we rounded the corner onto Mutanabbi Street, and I stopped short to take in the sight. Everywhere I looked there were books. It seemed like virtually every building on the street was a book store, and each one had tables full of paperbacks sitting outside. Stacks of books lay everywhere on the pavement, and I even saw some spread out over the hood of an old beat-up car. And there were nearly as many people as books, milling about and thumbing through worn paperbacks being resold for the tenth time. It was like a flea market on steroids.

We snaked our way through the crowd for a little more than a block and entered a small bookstore. It was a plain looking, tan building with only one small window and little in the way of advertisements on the outside. As the others entered, I stopped Sully and pointed at the white Arabic print on the faded brown sign above the entrance.

"The Comedy Bookstore," I said.

Sully looked at me curiously. "You speak Arabic?" he asked. I smiled wryly and entered the shop, happy to be the one withholding information for once.

Like the other stores, this one was also packed full of books on card tables and on shelves lining three walls. A young woman with a small child was browsing near the front as we entered, and a gangly teenage boy with a magazine lounged behind the cash register, chewing on an unlit cigarette. He greeted the group warmly, and I got the impression that they were not strangers to him. We loitered in the store making small talk, until the few customers present left.

The boy shut the front door and stood guard while Tank and Jackson slid a large bookshelf away from the back wall, revealing a doorway to a staircase. We quickly filed through the opening and down the stairs, sliding the bookcase back in place behind us.

"Where did you learn Arabic?" Sully asked as we descended under the city.

"I didn't." I was giving him a taste of his own medicine now, keeping him in suspense, and it was pretty clear that he didn't like it.

"Then how did you know what the sign said?"

"I have my ways," I smiled. In reality, I did not speak Arabic, and I had merely guessed at the meaning of the sign. It seemed like the logical thing for the bookstore to be called, knowing The Committee used it as a safe house.

At the bottom of the stairs, I stepped onto a landing and turned to find more stairs leading underground even further. "How far down does this go?" I asked.

"Just three flights," Jackson said, standing immediately to my right. He was impossible to see in the darkness, and when he spoke, I was startled by how close he was.

"We had to put it far enough underground so people in the buildings above can't hear us," he explained. So that meant that the underground safe house was below more than just the shop that doubled as an entrance. I was about to ask how many buildings they used as a roof, when we reached the bottom of the staircase, and I stepped down off of the hard cement steps onto a soft floor.

Lights were soon turned on, and I saw that we were standing in what appeared to be a large cave. It was maybe thirty feet square and roughly fifteen feet high. I looked down to see a red and tan ornamental rug under my feet, spanning the gap between the stairs and a sitting room that resembled the interior of the house back in Cuba. The large rug reminded me of the one I had admired in the Oval Office.

There were several leather couches and a chair situated around a dark, cherry colored coffee table. Just inside the room to my left and right sat two writing tables, and bookshelves lined two of the dirt walls. I couldn't be sure, but it certainly looked like these shelves even held the same books as the Cuba house. In the far corner of the spacious hideout was a small kitchenette with a stove and refrigerator. I looked up and saw a chandelier hanging from the dirt ceiling. I could only imagine how they had managed to run the electrical and safely suspend the large lighting fixture in dirt.

"This place is incredible," I mumbled to no one in particular.

"Yeah, it's not too bad," Jackson replied.

"All the comforts of home," Mickey added wryly.

"But where's the bathroom?"

Jackson smiled and motioned for me to follow him across the room. We walked past a large bookcase that appeared to be against the wall. However, once on the other side and looking back, I could see that it was actually set at an angle, with the far side about two feet out. Behind the bookcase there was an opening that led to a small cavity in the wall of the cave. I stepped through the gap and peaked inside the tiny room.

"Is that an airplane toilet?" I asked, recognizing it from my plane trips the day before.

"Yup," Jackson nodded. "It sucks."

"Well, you've got such nice furniture everywhere. Surely you can afford to get a better toilet."

He laughed. "No, I mean it's got a vacuum hooked up to it. It sucks everything out of the room and deposits it elsewhere."

"Oh, right. I see." It was quite ingenious really, since we were too far below ground to connect to the sewer system—although I was curious where the waste got "deposited."

We returned to the main room and I was surprised by a new face. At the bottom of the steps, a thin, Middle Eastern man in a wrinkled suit was speaking rapid Arabic with Mickey. He had shifty eyes and glanced around the room nervously as he spoke.

"Who's that?" I asked Jackson.

"I'm guessing it's Mickey's contact on the inside," he explained. Everyone moved to the couches and sat, so I followed suit. I now noticed that the boy from the book shop above was in the kitchenette pouring some sort of drinks for everyone. He delivered them on a tray while Mickey introduced his contact.

"Everyone, I would like you to meet Zaid Yusuf Uday. He is a chef at the royal palace." We nodded politely and mumbled various greetings. Mickey briefly introduced the members of the group— first names only, of course—while the bookstore kid made the rounds with his tray of drinks, and I politely took one. I inspected the small brownish-green glass beaker resting on a cheap china saucer. It appeared to be tea. I had never been a big fan, but didn't feel it would be appropriate not to drink. I already felt very much like an outsider in the group and was anxious to fit in, and I was thirsty.

"Zaid is familiar with the man we now know as Evan Brown," Mickey explained as I sipped my drink. It was very strong and very sweet, apparently loaded with sugar. I made a face and Jackson, sitting near me, smiled knowingly.

He leaned over and whispered, "That's how they drink it here; the sweeter, the better." I looked sheepishly around the room, hoping no one else had noticed my reaction.

Mickey, annoyed at being interrupted, glanced sideways at Jackson and then continued, "Zaid has been very helpful in the gathering of information. Mr. Brown spends a good deal of time at the palace, and we have learned that he owns a small house across the river. I've got all the details." He held up a manila folder with several papers inside.

"Alright, thank you, Zaid. You've been most helpful," Sully said, taking charge. Zaid took his cue to leave and politely excused himself. The boy left with him and when they were gone, we got down to business.

"So, what's the plan?" Jackson asked, impatiently.

"I think we split up," Sully decided.

"I'll go check out the house," Mickey offered.

Sully nodded. "Okay, I'll go with Mickey."

"I think I can handle it," Mickey protested. "It's just a little surveillance."

"No one goes anywhere alone," Sully ordered.

"What, you don't trust me?" Mickey argued. Sully ignored him.

"I'll go with Mickey to check out the house. Tank and Jackson, you take the newbie and do some surveillance at the palace—external only."

That was fine with me. I'd had enough excitement the night before, and sneaking into a nearly empty house in Havana was a far cry from infiltrating a fortified palace in the heart of a major city. "Each group takes a radio but remember, these things can be intercepted, so use it sparingly and code as much as possible."

I begrudgingly stood from the couch and returned my tea cup to the kitchen. I had been hoping for some rest, but clearly would not get any yet. The short nap on the plane had not been sufficient, and may have even made me more tired. A box was produced from under a couch and equipment was passed around. Each group packed a backpack with a walkie talkie and a 9mm "just in case".

We ascended the staircase and were thrust back into the chaos of the crowded street above. Tank, Jackson, and I returned to the van while Sully and Mickey walked the other direction down Mutanabbi Street, dissolving into the crowd.

Chapter 13

Even from the protection of a nearby building, Saddam Hussein's presidential palace was impressive. At six stories high, it towered above the surrounding structures. Numerous elaborate, open balconies protruded from various rooms, giving them the feel of high end condos back in the States. Together with its ornate gardens, the palace covered an entire city block and had a wonderful view of the mighty Tigris River as it snaked its way through the city.

I noticed several large stone structures placed around a modest lake in the front of the palace, which Jackson explained were fireplaces. "They look quite beautiful when they're all lit up at night," he commented. "I'm not real sure what the point is though, aside from decoration."

We could barely see the river from the abandoned office building in which we had set up a surveillance post. We could, however, see the rear entrance into the palace, which Zaid had said was used by many of the staff, including Mr. Brown.

"How hot does it get here?" I asked, sweating in the small room. After an hour, the space had become increasingly stuffy, and we were getting almost no crosswind through the open windows. The putrid smell of what we assumed was probably a dead rodent of sorts was finally starting to go away at least. Or maybe I had just gotten used to it.

"It's not unusual for it to hit 110 degrees," Jackson said, fanning himself with a piece of old cardboard he had found in a corner. There was a mysterious reddish brown stain on one side, and I wondered what sort of nasty things were being flung into the air.

"You Yanks are all a bunch of wimps," Tank teased. "This is just like summer back home in Texas."

"Who you callin' a Yank?" Jackson challenged. "I'm from Canada, remember?"

"It's still north."

"Yeah, well if Canadians are Yanks," he countered, "then you Texans are all dirty Mexicans."

"Wasn't your dad from New York?"

"So, what are the odds that we'll actually see Evan?" I asked, changing the subject.

Jackson shrugged. "I dunno. I'd say about 50/50. According to Mickey's source, Evan has been hanging around the palace quite a bit lately, so hopefully..."

"And if we do see him?" I inquired. Jackson looked to tank with raised eyebrows. Tank just smiled, made a fist with his right hand, and punched his open left hand. We all laughed, but I wasn't sure if he was really joking or not.

From what I could tell, we were watching some sort of service entrance, and though we had seen a few people enter and exit the mammoth structure, the place seemed fairly quiet. Looking through the high powered binoculars I had retrieved from the pack, I watched an elderly man carry a box of fresh fruits into the palace.

As he struggled to balance the box while opening the door, my mouth started to water, and I realized how hungry I was. We'd been so busy in Cuba, and now here in Iraq, that I hadn't had a chance to eat much. Right on cue, my stomach growled. Jackson heard it from his seat a few feet away and reached into the backpack, producing a banana. Though it was a little too ripe and sort of squishy, I quickly devoured it and felt much better.

I was about to ask if there was seconds, when our radio leaped to life, and the silence was broken by Sully's distorted voice, "We found the levis." I frowned, not understanding the code, but Tank and Jackson were too busy with the radio to notice.

"What's the place like?" Tank asked.

"Pretty empty," came the reply. "You'll never guess what's in the outer pocket, though."

"What?"

"Well... let's just say Mickey's got the sniffles." At this, Tank and Jackson's eyes widened, and they leaned toward the radio, listening more intently.

"Are you saying he has a cold?" Tank asked.

"Yup, and it's a massive one."

"How big?"

"Not sure yet, but it's definitely the worst I've ever seen."

The two just sat stunned for a moment, while I tried desperately to understand what was going on. Finally Jackson grabbed the radio eagerly, "Do you need some help?"

"No, you stay there," came the reply. "Keep an eye out for the target. We'll do the same here. We can deal with the cold later."

"Alright. Sounds good. Keep us informed."

"Will do."

Once the conversation was over, I asked them to translate for me. "So, I'm lost. What's going on?" I was beginning to see how this code would be very difficult to decipher in another language. I spoke English, and I still couldn't figure out what they were talking about.

Jackson laughed. "Well, they said they were at the levis, which are made by Levi Strauss, rhyming with house, and that they found something in the 'outer pocket', which is a combo of outer space and pocket lint, meaning 'basement'."

"Okay, but what's with all the talk of Mickey getting a cold?"

Jackson raised his eyebrows and smiled mischievously, "They were saying they found gold."

"Gold?"

"Yeah, that's why we were so interested," Tank added. "Sully said it's the most he's ever seen."

"Really? I guess the luck of the Irish really does work," I teased.

"Yeah, the little leprechaun finally found that gold at the end of the rainbow," Tank added in his best Irish accent.

"You know, for years there have been rumors that Hitler's gold wasn't all recovered after World War II," Jackson said. "I've heard theories that he sent large caches to various places around the world to protect it."

"So, you think maybe this Evan character is stashing Nazi gold at his house?" I asked.

"Yeah, that would make sense," Tank said. "We've seen Castro with Nazi gold in Havana before. Why wouldn't they be using it here too?"

"So, are we going to... um... confiscate it?" I asked.

"Of course."

Chapter 14

 half hour later, the excitement of the gold had worn off, and heat and boredom were lulling me to sleep, when Jackson suddenly jumped from his chair and moved to the window for a better look.

"Guys, I think that might be him," he declared, and Tank and I quickly joined him with our binoculars.

After adjusting the focus and locating the rear palace entrance in the eyepiece, I saw a middle-aged man with a thick beard who looked very much like the grainy photo Mickey had shown us the day before. But he also looked a lot like the rest of the people that

I had seen entering and leaving the palace in the past few hours. The main difference was that this guy wore a nice suit and jewelry, as opposed to the service workers we had seen previously.

"Are you sure?" I asked, skeptically.

"Yeah, it's him," Tank declared. "I can see the scar on his forehead." I thought back to the day before, but couldn't remember any scar in the picture.

"There was a scar on the guy in the photo?" I asked skeptically.

"Yeah, right up near the hairline," Jackson corroborated. "You didn't see it?" I didn't want to confirm my ignorance, so I simply said nothing. Instead I stared through the window as our target paused in the garden to light a cigarette. He glanced around briefly and proceeded south down the street away from the palace.

Jackson was shaking his head now. "I told George you weren't Committee material, but he insisted."

"Because I missed a scar in a crappy picture?" I snapped.

Tank smiled and shook his head as he loaded the binoculars in the backpack, suddenly hurrying to leave. "You couldn't see it in the picture. Mickey told us about the scar the other day, before you showed up." Jackson looked hurt that Tank had ended his fun. "Apparently it was an unsuccessful assassination attempt a few years ago by the Bumbles. Didn't kill him, but they did leave their mark."

"What are you going to do?" I asked, adding my binoculars to the pack. Jackson repeated the punching motion Tank had done earlier, and this time I got the impression that they were serious.

"You're just gonna jump him out in the open?" That didn't seem like a great plan. Wasn't this group all about secrecy?

"Don't worry, it'll be easy." Tank hefted the bag over his shoulder and left the room. Jackson took one more quick look at Evan through the window, and he and I followed the big guy out the door.

In the mid-afternoon heat, the street was nearly deserted. I saw a couple kids kicking a soccer ball back and forth a few blocks away. They seemed bored with the game, and I thought perhaps that ball had crossed the street a few too many times.

An odd squeaking sound caught my attention, and I turned to see an elderly shop owner cleaning the windows on his store front. I couldn't read the sign, in Arabic of course, but the shelves inside appeared to be holding loaves of bread, so I assumed it was probably a bakery. In an instant my hunger returned again.

Jackson grabbed my arm and led me across the street into an alley while Tank jogged about a hundred yards to the south, away from the palace and the approaching Evan. Tucked away in the alley, I saw a fire escape above us, and realized that although it was a cloudless day, we would be hidden in the shadows fairly well.

Before long, Evan made his way down the street and was quickly approaching our location. Jackson stood up straight, leaning against the building just inside the alley, and indicated that I should hide behind a nearby dumpster. As we waited, I noticed a small plastic syringe in Jackson's left hand with a short needle protruding from the end. I wanted to ask him what was in the syringe, but knew that I needed to stay quiet.

Suddenly, Tank appeared on the sidewalk, carrying a large cardboard box. He paused just outside the alley to reposition the weight in his arms. At that exact instant, Evan came into view from the other direction and sidestepped to avoid Tank and his cumbersome load. For a brief moment he was in the shadows of the alley and before he even knew anything was happening, Jackson pounced.

With one well-synchronized motion, his left hand raised the syringe, and his right arm slid under Evan's shoulder and around his chest. In less than a second, the syringe was in his neck, and Jackson was dragging him behind the dumpster where I was hiding. His entire body hung limp.

"What the hell!?" I exclaimed. "Is he dead?" Jackson just frowned and shushed me. Tank entered the alley and tossed the box to the side. It bounced gently, and it was obvious that the seemingly heavy container was actually empty.

I was elected to retrieve the van and quickly jogged down the street to another alley where we had stashed it several hours earlier. There were now four boys kicking the soccer ball, and it appeared the beginnings of a pickup game were taking shape as a fifth child set up milk crates as goals.

The shop owner was nowhere to be found, but I spotted a woman in full Islamic dress, covering all but her eyes, walking toward us from the south. She was several blocks away, and I felt certain that she could not have seen anything. And if she had... well, hopefully we wouldn't be here much longer anyway.

Entering the vehicle, I took several deep breaths, reached up, and slid the shifter down until I felt it click into the notch. I eased onto the gas and heard a crunch as the car lurched backward. *What an idiot*, I thought. *D for Drive, R for Reverse.* You'd think I'd never driven a car before.

Fearing the worst, I checked the mirror and saw a dumpster rolling slowly down the alley away from the van. It came to a rest about ten feet away, and I breathed a sigh of relief that it hadn't caused any damage or been louder. I seriously doubted that my car insurance back home covered this type of situation.

I found drive, and the van started slowly, then sprang to life when I gave it a little gas. I tried to relax and drive nonchalantly down the street to the alley, as if I travelled the same route every day. I finally emerged onto the street and rolled safely to where Jackson and Tank were waiting impatiently. I pulled the van all the way up against the curb, hoping to block the view into the alley as much as possible.

As I jumped out and rounded the van to open the side door, Tank and Jackson emerged from the shadows carrying the large box. No acting was required this time, as the box really was heavy. It quickly became obvious that the package was not going to fit through the side, so I closed the door and opened the back hatch instead. I tried to ignore the obtrusive dent in the center of the back bumper and hoped no one else would notice it either.

After pulling on several levers, I finally found the correct one, and the back row of seats folded down flat, allowing the boxed up Nazi to be quickly tossed in. The doors were shut, and the three of us stood around for a moment chatting as if we were bored with our routine deliveries. Satisfied that no one was watching, we piled into the van and returned to Mutanabbi Street, monitoring our mirrors the whole way for signs of anyone who might be following us.

Late in the day now, the book shops were beginning to pack up their displays in the street. There were still plenty of people browsing, but not enough to prevent us from driving up to The Comedy Bookstore instead of parking around the corner. Jackson and Tank unloaded the box of "books" from the van and into the safe house underground.

"How long is he gonna be out?" I asked. Evan was still unconscious as Tank tightened the ropes holding him to the chair.

"A half hour, maybe," Jackson said. "I gave him 50 mg of Propofol." So now he was a doctor too?

"Is that safe?"

He shrugged. "Sure, let's say it is."

Before I could inquire further, the radio erupted again. This time it was Mickey, and he sounded panicked and out of breath. Through the static we heard his distorted voice pant, "Help! They... know what... dead."

Tank grabbed the radio. "Mickey, you're coming through very distorted. Say again?" We waited eagerly but heard only silence.

"Mickey!" Tank shouted. "We did not copy. Repeat your last transmission." More silence followed, and I was about to suggest ascending the stairs for a better signal, when Mickey's voice returned to the speaker, this time loud and clear.

"They killed him!"

Chapter 15

Jackson catapulted across the room and snatched the radio out of Tank's hand.

"What? Who?" he shouted into the receiver.

"Sully," came the breathless reply.

"What? Who killed him? What happened?"

"It was Evan. He came in the back door and surprised us." We all turned to look at the unconscious man we had abducted outside the palace, and I began to wonder if we had made a mistake. "I took a bullet in the arm and managed to escape," Mickey continued, "but Sully took two in the chest." In the background we heard shouts followed by two more gun shots, and the radio went dead.

"Mickey!" Jackson screamed. "Mickey!"

No response.

"Dammit!" the radio flew across the room, crashing into a wall and sending dirt particles flying everywhere.

In a flash, Jackson retrieved another syringe from a bag under the couch. This was promptly, and carelessly, injected into the man whose identity was now in question. After a few seconds his eyes flicked open, and he looked quickly around the room, clearly confused and frightened. Before he could say anything, Jackson was in his face.

"Who are you?" he demanded.

Wide eyed, the man responded in heavily accented, broken English, "My... my name, Samir."

"Samir? You sure about that?"

"Yes... sure," he stammered, nodding his head emphatically. Great. Now we had kidnapped some random Iraqi citizen. What the hell were we supposed to do with him? We couldn't just drive him back to the palace and say, "Oops, our bad. Sorry."

"Where'd you get the scar, Samir?" Jackson demanded, giving the disfigurement a quick smack with the back of his palm. Samir hesitated for only a second, but it was enough to show he was thinking of a lie.

"It was... I..."

"Don't lie to me," Jackson threatened. "We know who you are, Mr. Brown."

Samir frowned. "Who?"

"Evan Brown, the son of Adolf and Eva Hitler." Jackson was holding nothing back.

The confusion that now formed on the man's face seemed sincere. "Hitler?" he asked slowly.

Tank stepped in next to Jackson now, and his substantial presence had its intended effect on the subject. He had apparently not seen the giant standing off to the side and leaned back, suddenly realizing the amount of damage that might be inflicted upon him.

"Who was it?" Tank bellowed, the gentleness gone from his voice. Our prisoner just shook his head, either unable or unwilling to answer. "My friend was killed at your house by one of your men," Tank continued, a large finger stabbing into the man's chest. "Now who was it?"

Samir was looking around the room again, but this time with a look of recognition. His shoulders relaxed and he laughed nervously. "The comedy?" he asked in perfect English. Now Tank and Jackson were shocked and took a step back.

"What do you know about it?" Jackson demanded, but the authority in his voice was faltering.

"Guys, I'm on your side." The accent was completely gone now, and I thought the man might even be American. "The name's Sam Russo, and I'm on The Committee."

"Bull," Tank declared without conviction.

"Call the President. He'll confirm it." Then, as an afterthought added, "Tell him you've got Carl Lewis in custody."

"I thought you said your name was Sam," I challenged.

"It is," he nodded calmly, "but George told me I was to come over here and be like Carl Lewis; you know, get the gold?"

Jackson eyed him suspiciously as he hesitantly retrieved the sat phone. Luckily the bookstore was now closed, because he had to ascend the stairs in order to use the phone, and he was in no mood to wait for customers to clear out. Tank paced the room scowling at Sam, or Evan, or Samir, or Carl, or whatever his real name was, as I searched the kitchen for some food.

"Where you from?" Tank snarled. He looked like he was trying to find something to destroy. *We need a punching bag down here*, I thought, and then realized I had said 'we' and flashed back to Sully's declaration that I would for sure join the Committee. Maybe he was right.

"Chicago," the interrogee replied.

"Sure you are," Tank snorted. "North side or south side?"

"North."

Tank stopped suddenly and studied the man. "Cubs or Sox?"

I could see where he was going with this. If our prisoner wasn't from the U.S., he most likely wouldn't know which team was from which part of the city.

"Cubs all the way," he declared confidently.

"Yeah, it was a 50/50 chance," Tank dismissed with a wave of his hand.

"I bet you were pretty excited when they made the World Series last year then," I offered, returning from the kitchen with a granola bar.

"I wish they had," he shrugged, "but San Francisco was too tough." Okay, so maybe he was telling the truth. The year before, the Cubs had lost the pennant to the Giants.

"Alright," Tank said, calming a bit, "so you like baseball. That doesn't mean anything."

Jackson came bounding down the stairs. "Untie him." He sounded slightly disappointed.

"What?" Tank exclaimed, still doubtful.

"George confirmed everything he said. He's Committee."

With a sigh, Tank began releasing the knots. No apologies were attempted. "So, what are you doing here in Baghdad?"

"I've been undercover in Saddam's government since last fall," Sam explained, rubbing his wrists.

"In Saddam's government?" I asked. "That sounds rather vague."

"I'm not exactly sure what my position is," he explained. "It changes somewhat from day to day. Mostly, I... help him procure things."

"Such as?"

"Anything, really. Guns, big screen televisions, women. Whatever he needs."

"To what end?" Jackson asked.

"Gold."

"Like Carl Lewis?" I offered.

Sam laughed. "Right. Saddam has a large stockpile of gold somewhere. My job was to get close to him and find out where." We all exchanged looks and he noticed. "What?"

"The gold is in your basement," Tank declared.

"What? I don't have a basement. I live in an apartment up north." If he was committee, why was he still lying to us?

"What about your house across the river?" I challenged.

Sam shrugged. "I don't have a house."

Jackson frowned, "Maybe Mickey's contact was feeding us bad information. Tank, do you still have that address? I think we'd better check out this house for ourselves. Something's up."

Chapter 16

The two-story stone residence was average sized by Iraqi standards. The home appeared to be well-maintained, and although not on the river per se, the water was visible from the property. A newer tan Cadillac sat in the driveway, which was lined with manicured bushes.

After circling the block once to see what we were dealing with, we parked around the corner and approached the building on foot. Retrieving pistols from the back of the van, the four of us formed a plan of attack. We didn't know what, or who, waited for us inside, but Mickey was in trouble, and the house was our only lead at the moment.

Sam and Jackson decided that they would go in the front, while Tank and I went around back. For once, I was in total agreement with the plan; I felt safer with the big guy nearby. Not that sneaking into a house in Baghdad could ever really be safe, but at least we would probably have the size advantage. It was better than nothing.

We entered cautiously with guns drawn. I nervously checked the safety for the tenth time—it was still off. While I had shot a gun before, my experience was extremely limited, and I definitely did not feel comfortable carrying around the pistol they had provided me. But I also knew that Sully could still be alive and dying inside, so what other choice did I have?

Sure, The Committee left the military stuff to the military, but no president with half a brain would send the Marines into a foreign country to rescue someone who wasn't supposed to be there and didn't technically even work for the government. We were his only hope.

The house appeared to be deserted, but we moved silently from room to room anyway, just to be safe. A modest kitchen with thick granite countertops showed no visible signs of having been used recently. Apart from a wood block with several large knives, the counters were bare. I considered taking one of the knives but figured I would probably just end up injuring myself. As little experience as I had with guns, I had even less with knives. Unless my

opponent was a carrot or a cardboard box, a knife was
going to do me little good.

We moved on to the open living space
adjacent to the kitchen, which contained only a large
ornamental multicolored rug resting on the floor in
front of a worn, dark blue couch. It certainly appeared
that no one was currently living in the house. After
checking a small empty room off of the great room,
probably some sort of den, we met Jackson and Sam at
the bottom of the stairs. They had found nothing but
open space and a few small pieces of furniture on the
second level as well.

We moved as a group to the basement stairs,
and Tank took the lead as we descended, weary of
what we might find.

"This is it," Sam whispered behind me.

"What?" I asked.

"The gold. This is where Saddam keeps his
gold. I've seen pictures of this staircase."

Reaching the bottom, we found that the
basement was one large room with concrete block
walls and a cement floor. It was completely empty,
except for a Nazi flag hanging on the far wall—a
simple red background with a black swastika
circumscribed by a white circle in the center. That
seemed to be a good indication that we were on the
right track, but any gold that may have been in the
basement before, was clearly now gone. We wandered
around a bit and pretended to inspect the space
anyway, just to be sure.

"This looks like the room I saw in the pictures," Sam said to no one in particular.

"How can you tell?" Jackson challenged. "It's just an empty room."

"Yeah, but you see how the wall over here is water stained? That's just like in the photos I saw. And I remember that carpet on the stairs." Sam explained that he had been snooping through some of Saddam's things a couple months earlier and found some old pictures of a group of Arabs carrying gold bars into the basement of a house. He said the bars in the photos were stamped with the Nazi swastika. "Remember, my job was to find this place," he added. "I paid attention to every detail in those pictures."

Jackson wasn't convinced, but let it go anyway. "Well, the gold is gone now," he said and began to ascend the stairs again with Sam close behind. I was about to do the same, when I noticed Tank standing in the center of the room, turning around in circles, clearly troubled by something.

"What is it?" I prodded.

He turned to face us. "The room isn't big enough," he declared.

"What do you mean?" Sam asked.

"Well, usually a basement would be the same size as the building above it, but this house probably extends another twenty feet that way." He pointed at the wall with the flag. We all processed this for a second and simultaneously realized what it meant— there was another room.

Crossing the cold cement floor, I ripped the flag off the wall, revealing a hole about three feet in diameter where several cement blocks were missing. I hesitated for a second, my instincts telling me not to let a flag touch the ground, then I remembered what flag I was holding and tossed it in a heap in the corner.

We quickly scrambled through the opening and into a smaller room, also with cement block walls. Slumped on the floor just to the right of the doorway was Sully's lifeless body, lying on his back. His shirt was stained red at the chest, and a small pool of blood had gathered under him. Following me through the hole, Sam moved immediately to the neck and checked for a pulse.

"He's gone," he proclaimed solemnly. "I'm sorry."

We stood in silence for a moment, and I pondered yet again whether I had made a terrible mistake by accepting the offer from the President. Deep down, I had known from the start that the job involved real danger; it was just easier to lie to myself. But lying was no longer an option now. One of my new partners, and someone I was beginning to consider a friend and mentor, lay dead on the floor in front of me.

I had never seen a dead body up close before, and despite the shock and horror I probably should have felt, it all seemed somehow routine. I guess it was because the body was not unexpected; Mickey had told us he was dead, and the scene was only confirming what we already knew. Aside from the blood, Sully appeared peaceful, as if he were sleeping.

Unfortunately, there was no time for mourning, no time for the depression of losing someone close. Mickey was still out there somewhere, on the run and in danger of joining Sully. And as uncomfortable as it felt, we also had to deal with the problem of a dead American in Baghdad. We weren't even supposed to be in the country, let alone in Saddam's secret underground vault.

Sam finally broke the silence. "Something's not right here."

"You mean, besides the fact that our friend is dead?" Jackson snapped.

"No, I mean look at where the body is. He's just inside the door, but off to the side, which means the shooter was in the room. Didn't you say that they were already here, waiting for someone to show up?" He was right. If Sully and Mickey were hiding in the room, they would have probably been shot by someone in the main part of the basement, or at least someone standing at the hole in the wall. How could anyone have surprised them that well?

"So, what are you saying?" Jackson didn't like the implication that Sully was dead due to his own incompetence.

Sam crossed the small room and began inspecting the cement block. Leaning in for a close look, he rubbed his hand along the wall a couple feet, and then stopped suddenly. He produced a large hunting knife from a back pocket and slid it into the wall along the edge of one of the blocks. It went in easily.

"There's a door here," he declared. The rest of us studied the wall closer. Sure enough, there was a small crack along the mortar, running all the way to the ground.

"But how do we open it?" I asked. Jackson and I began knocking and feeling the wall for any abnormal features. About halfway down, a block moved a little when I pushed against it. I pushed harder, and it slid several inches into the wall, revealing a notch in the side of the block next to it. Jackson did the same with a block about three feet away laterally, and soon we were each pulling on a handle of sorts. A cutout section of the wall slid noisily and slowly on hidden tracks into the room, uncovering a long unlit tunnel.

"This must be how they were ambushed," Tank observed. I wondered if he was thinking clearly in light of the situation, and apparently I wasn't the only one who didn't agree with his assessment.

"I dunno," Sam argued, "that thing sure makes a lot of noise, and it doesn't move very quickly. I doubt it would really surprise anyone in the room... unless they were deaf."

"Well, how do you explain it then?" Tank countered. Sam just shook his head, knowing any hypothesis offered would only offend his new companions.

"So, what's our next move?" I asked, changing the subject.

"Well, the gold is gone, and you're down a man, so I guess I'm with you guys now," Sam said.

"We've got to find Mickey." Jackson was taking charge. "Assuming he's still alive."

"And we need to get rid of the body," Sam added, receiving harsh glares from Tank and Jackson. He held up his hands in defense. "Look guys. I'm sorry about your friend. I understand. But an American cannot be found down here. That's all there is to it."

"And what do you suggest?" Tank challenged.

"We drag him upstairs and burn the house."

"What?" exclaimed Jackson. "After all he's done for his country, not to mention me personally, we're just gonna leave him here?"

"We have no choice. Even if we could get his body out and somehow sneak it back to the safe house, we'll never be able to get him out of the country and back to the states without being seen," Sam argued. "Come on, think logically. You know this is the right move. That's the whole point of The Committee; we think logically and use our brains. None of this 'no man left behind' junk—risking our lives to bring a dead body home." He was still receiving only glares, but no one was objecting either. "We're not the Marines. If it was you on the floor there, would you want the rest of your team to risk becoming dead bodies themselves just to bring you home and bury you in the dirt? If he were alive, it'd be a different story—I'd climb a mountain to save him—but a dead body is just that, a dead body."

He had a point. It wasn't like Sully needed his body now that he was dead. I had always felt that funerals and burying people in coffins was more for the family and friends who were still alive then for the dead guy. Jackson broke his stare and searched the room for another option.

Sam bent down next to Sully's motionless body. "Think of it as... a cremation. I'll take care of it. You guys wait here. Once the place is lit up, we'll sneak out through the tunnel." Jackson nodded slowly and joined Tank, who had chosen not to respond, instead turning his focus on the tunnel and the unique door that disguised its location. I watched as Sam strained to lift Sully up over his shoulder and carefully hauled him through the opening and toward the stairs.

"Sam, wait!" I exclaimed, and quickly climbed through the hole. Retrieving the flag from the corner I tossed it over his other shoulder. "While you're at it, burn this too." He nodded and disappeared up the steps. I climbed back through and noticed how large the pool of blood looked now that the body was gone.

"I never thought it would be possible to hate the Nazis even more," I commented, staring at the smeared blood where Sully had been laying. Although I had known him for little more than a day, I was beginning to feel like part of the team, and the enemy had stolen our leader.

"Yup, that's what they're good at," Tank said, retrieving flashlights from his backpack while diverting his eyes from the large pool of blood. "Creating hate."

I could hear Sam moving furniture around upstairs, and I shifted my attention to the tunnel and our impending exit. But as I turned to cross the room, the referee in my brain threw another flag, and my subconscious made me look back. There was something peculiar about the blood smear. I paused and turned my head to the side trying to get the correct viewing angle. Next to the wall, it had been hidden from view by Sully's body, but now that he was upstairs on the bonfire, it was clear as day.

Scrawled in the pool of red was a distorted four leaf clover, and directly above it, a solitary letter "A".

Chapter 17

I tilted my head to one side, then the other, unsure if I was really seeing the smudges clearly. "Guys, you need to see this," I called over my shoulder.

"What?" Jackson asked from the covert opening in the wall behind me.

"I think Sully left us a note."

The tunnel was abruptly abandoned as both men quickly joined me and began tilting their heads as well. I flashed back to the meeting with the President the day before. *I need someone who is unencumbered by outside influences and has an unbiased view of the situation.* Had he known there was a traitor in the group?

"I don't believe it," Jackson declared. "How could he..." he trailed off, not wanting to say the words out loud.

"All of our info came from him," I reminded them. "It was his contact with the Bumbles. He surveyed the Castro house. Zaid was his guy on the inside at the palace. He could have told us anything he wanted."

Tank was nodding now. "He's right. We know his info on Evan was wrong. Hell, not only is Sam not a Nazi, he's Committee. What are the odds of that?"

As we pondered the question, Sam returned to the basement and found us still staring at the blood smears. "Is that what I think it is?" he asked, breaking us out of our trance. Our silence confirmed his suspicion. "But what's with the clubs?" he asked.

"It's a clover," Tank corrected. "The missing member of our group is affectionately known as 'Mickey', because he looks Irish."

"So, the recovery mission has become a man hunt," Jackson sighed. Mickey was now a marked man, and Jackson and Tank had just lost two of their closest friends within a couple hours. I couldn't imagine what was going through their minds.

"There is one other possibility we must consider," Sam offered. "What if Sully was the traitor? Mickey found out, shot him, and Sully smeared the note to throw us off."

"No," Tank shook his head, "not Sully."

"I'm just saying it's possible."

"No, it's not," Tank insisted.

"Well, either way we've got to find Mickey," I interrupted. Arguing about it wasn't going to solve anything.

Tank sighed and glanced somberly up toward the cremation in progress above us. "If it's alright with everyone, I think we ought to say a few words for Sully first."

No one objected, and Jackson offered to go first. "We all know Sully was dedicated to his service and to his country. He was a good man and a great leader. He committed no sin and did not deserve this ending. Sorry we couldn't give you a proper burial, boss. But know that we're gonna get the traitor. Justice will be served." Jackson looked to me, and I cleared my throat as I searched for the right words.

"I only just met Sully yesterday, but I already considered him a friend. He was accepting and patient with me, quickly dismissing my moments of doubt. He will be missed, both as a leader and a friend." I looked to Tank, who briefly bowed his head and made the sign of the cross on his chest.

"I have done what is righteous and just; do not leave me to my oppressors. My eyes fail, looking for your salvation, looking for your righteous promise. Deal with your servant according to your love. Give me discernment that I may understand your statutes. It is time for you to act, O LORD; your law is being broken. Our brother has been assigned a grave with the enemy in his death, though no deceit was in his mouth. Father, into your hands we commit this spirit."

"Amen. And now we've got to get out of this house," Sam declared. "The whole place is gonna be ashes in a few minutes." With that, he stepped on the bloody note and twisted his foot, erasing the message.

Flashlight in hand, he charged down the tunnel. I quickly followed after him as Tank and Jackson slid the door back into place, closing off our escape route from the flames.

Chapter 18

ith the opening blocked, the space suddenly felt smaller in the darkness. I was glad we had the flashlights and began sweeping mine back and forth, looking for unknown monsters that might be lurking underground. We followed what we hoped was an eventual exit for a good half mile, through twists, dips, rises, and even a few stairs. Finally, I saw a light in the distance. None of us knew where the tunnel would lead, and we approached the light slowly and cautiously.

As we neared the illumination, we found that it actually came from an opening in the ceiling covered by a grate, and that the tunnel continued on further. We decided it would be best to exit the underground passageway as soon as possible, and Tank volunteered to climb up and investigate. We boosted him up—no small feat—and the grate was easily removed.

After quickly evaluating the space and finding no impending doom, he motioned for us to follow. I soon found myself climbing into a small cement room with only three walls. A small flower bed sat just outside the opening and after a brief moment of confusion, I realized it was one of the fireplaces I had seen in front of the palace earlier.

"We're back at the palace?" I asked, incredulous.

"Apparently," Sam shrugged. "I knew Saddam had tunnels running all over the place under Baghdad, but I've never been down here."

"Well, at least we know where we are," Jackson observed. "It'll be dark soon. I think we should get back to the bookstore and call George. If Mickey took off with the gold, we've got precious little time to catch up with him before he disappears for good."

Although free from our underground confinement, we now had the difficult task of crossing the palace garden without being seen. We waited for several long minutes in the small structure but saw and heard no one, so we decided to make our move. Jackson exited the front of the fireplace and did an awkward looking crouch run to a large well-manicured shrub about twenty feet away. From a squatting position, he leaned forward into the bush, partly to conceal himself in the leaves and also so he could see through the other side.

Satisfied that the coast was clear, he motioned for us to follow. I wasn't so sure that was a good idea. I'd seen enough movies to know the first guy always makes it through. Then the sniper identifies where the people are and picks off the next runner. I also knew there probably weren't any snipers sitting around waiting to shoot people crossing the royal gardens, but that didn't seem to steady my shaking hands any.

Half expecting bullets to rain down on me, I ran with Tank past Jackson's bush and down a row of tulips. We practically crashed into another bush, and I realized I was breathing much too hard for the short distance I had just run. I tried to slow my respiration and listen for any movement close by, while glancing wildly in all directions. I saw nothing but a peaceful, innocent garden.

With that one dash, we had traversed nearly half of the garden without incident, and I began to think that my fears had been unfounded. I managed to calm slightly, although my heart and lungs did not, while next to me, Tank motioned for Jackson and Sam to move further toward safety. They began another ridiculous looking low run past the tulips and turned the corner at a large pear tree covered in white flowers.

Suddenly, I saw a small door open on the side of the palace. It appeared to be another service entrance—just a plain metal door with no markings— but the group of men exiting looked like anything but servants. Three were dressed in full military uniforms and carried Ak-47s over their shoulders and pistols on their hips. The other two, in the center of the group, wore typical Muslim robes and head dresses, and strolled leisurely. There was an obvious air of importance about them.

I quickly whistled my best bird impersonation, hoping to alert them before they were spotted by the men with guns. I was gripped with terror momentarily as I wondered if the bird I was imitating was indigenous to Iraq. Perhaps the men would be alarmed by a bird call they were not familiar with. By trying to help, I may have just made things worse.

But the moment passed, and I realized that it was a preposterous idea anyway. Sure enough, the men made no indication that they had even heard me, let alone were distressed by the sound.

Recognizing the whistle for what it was, Jackson immediately became intimate with the ground and rolled to his right off of the path. Following suit, Sam ducked behind a pear tree and carefully watched the men. After a few seconds, his eyes lit up with recognition and he turned to Tank and I, who were still trying to remain one with the bush.

Sam nodded toward the group that was making its way into the garden and, it appeared, was slowly heading our direction. He then reached up and grabbed his chest while cupping his hands. It seemed like he was trying to sign 'breasts'. I hadn't the slightest idea what that could mean.

"Is he saying one of them is a woman?" I whispered, barely audible. I wasn't even sure if I made any noise at first, but I didn't dare speak any louder. Tank either heard me or read my lips, because he responded with a slight shake of the head, offering no explanation. Sam then pointed at himself, the imminent danger, and gave a thumbs up sign. Tank nodded his understanding, and Sam abandoned his hiding place, jogging down the path toward the men.

"What's he doing?" I hissed. Tank frowned and his eyebrows rose slightly into a stern glare. The message was clear, "shut up". I returned my attention to Sam, who was now talking to the important men inside the safety of the three guards. He was very animated with lots of hand gestures and pointed across the river at the city. I turned to look and noticed for the first time a large amount of billowing smoke rising skyward in front of the setting sun. This was, no doubt, coming from the improvised cremation at the former hiding place of Saddam's Nazi gold.

When my gaze returned to the garden scene, Sam was walking briskly back to the palace with the important men, and the guards were close behind. We completed our leap-frogging the rest of the way out of danger without further incident, and began strolling down a deserted city street, hoping not to stand out.

It was eerily quiet. I was familiar with big cities, and there were always people around. But somehow I saw not a single person or car anywhere. I couldn't understand why the streets were so empty. "Where is everyone?"

"Maghrib," Jackson explained. "Evening prayers at sunset." Of course. A concept that was foreign to us Americans, nearly the whole of the Middle East prayed together five times a day. As a good Lutheran, I prayed on Sundays at church and before meals when visiting my folks back in Iowa. That added up to maybe five times per month, not per day. I had noticed my quota going up since embarking on my crazy adventure though.

"So, is Sam gonna be alright?" I asked.

"Sure, he's worked his way into Saddam's circle, remember? They think he's one of them." I still wasn't convinced, but nodded anyway. Who was I to argue? And I had more pressing things to ask about.

"Okay, so you gotta explain the sign language to me."

Tank laughed. "He said he's thinking about getting implants, and I said he should go for it, so he went to ask Saddam if he would help pay for them."

"No, really," I chuckled.

"He was saying that one of the men in the garden was Saddam," Jackson offered.

"Saddam has breasts?"

"No, but a madam does."

I suddenly remembered the rhyming slang. "Ah, I see, so Saddam is madam?"

"Right."

"So, how are we getting back to the safe house?" I asked as we passed by a small white Chevy Caprice with no windows and several bullet holes on the passenger side. Tank shrugged with a mischievous smile and opened the passenger door of the car. He then leaned across the seat to reach under the steering column.

"Say a little prayer," he said with a smile. I did just that and within thirty seconds, the car roared to life.

"You're gonna have to teach me how to do that sometime," I told Tank.

"Get in," Jackson commanded, and we were soon speeding through the deserted streets of downtown Baghdad once again.

Chapter 19

J ackson tossed the satellite phone to me, and I looked at it hesitantly as if it might explode.

"You want *me* to call him?" I asked doubtfully.

"Tank and I have other things we need to do. This place is compromised now. We've got to clear it out."

"But I don't..." I started.

"Look," Jackson snapped, "Sully is dead, Sam is otherwise occupied at the palace, and Mickey is a treasonous bastard who cares more about gold than his country. That leaves Tank and I as the only ones who know how to clean this place of all evidence that

Americans have been here so that we can avoid starting World War III. Just make the damn call."

His outburst shocked me back to reality, and I suddenly realized how trivial my problems were compared to theirs. I was nervous about making a phone call and delivering bad news; they had just lost two good friends and were trying to prevent an international incident.

I left them to their work and reascended the stairs to The Comedy Bookstore. It was nearly dark outside now, and the shop had been closed early on our return, so I had complete privacy.

I crisscrossed the room briefly until I located a corner that provided the strongest signal and typed in the numbers provided by Jackson. After some beeps and clicks, I was surprised to hear the voice of President Bush on the other end.

"How's it going over there?" he asked pleasantly, apparently knowing where the call came from.

"Uh... fine, sir," I blurted out. Everything was, of course, not fine, but I had expected to talk to a secretary first and figure out what to say while she connected me to the Oval Office. Hearing his voice caught me by surprise.

"Good to hear."

"Well, actually no," I backtracked. "Not fine. Um... there's been a bit of a complication."

"What happened?" he inquired, sounding more annoyed than concerned. I could hear people talking in the background and wondered if he was really listening to me. Surely he hadn't answered the phone during some sort of meeting, had he?

"Sully's dead."

There was a slight pause, and then I heard a hand snapping on the other end, and the background voices disappeared. When he finally spoke, the friendliness was gone. "Solomon? How?"

"Well, he was shot."

"By Evan?"

"I'm not sure there even is an Evan." More silence from Washington. "You still there, sir?" I heard a sharp intake of breath, as if I had awaken him from a trance.

"Yes," he said finally. "You'd better tell me everything."

I very briefly covered the main points of the day's events, including Sully's death, the note revealing Mickey as the traitor, and Sam saving us in the garden. He responded with a loud sigh.

"Okay. So, what's our exposure here?"

"Um... exposure, sir?"

"Does anyone know you guys are there?"

I hadn't expected the question, and I had to stop and consider for a moment. "I don't think so. The fire should have disposed of Sully's body. The only question is who Mickey is working with. But considering that we think he took the gold, I doubt he's in contact with Saddam."

"And you guys are safe?"

149

Having escaped the tunnels and Saddam's garden, I felt like we were reasonably out of harm's way. It occurred to me now though, that the bookstore might not be secure anymore.

"I think we're okay for now. I doubt Mickey is gonna stick around. I'm guessing he'll be out of the country as soon as possible."

"Probably," he agreed. "And once he's gone it will be hard to find him."

"No doubt."

His tone became authoritative suddenly, indicating that he was ready to end the conversation. "Okay. Well, tell the others to close the bookstore and clean everything up."

"They're already working on it," I assured him, and then hesitated before moving on to what I had been pondering since we found Sully's message. "Sir... you knew this was going to happen, didn't you?"

He ignored the question. "Good, well thanks for the update, Caleb. I'm gonna have a satellite search done of the area and see if we can get a location on Brenton. Why don't you guys call back in fifteen minutes and I'll update you on what we've found."

With that, the line went dead.

Although he hadn't answered my question, I felt like I had received a confirmation. His non-answer could only be interpreted as an affirmation. Unless of course he hadn't heard me ask it. We were talking across the globe on a satellite phone. But still, something told me that he knew there was a traitor in the group. The timing of my recruitment just before Mickey's treason was too coincidental.

I knew I should have been angry about being put into a dangerous situation without all the facts, but for some reason I felt more flattered than anything. The President had needed someone he could count on to not turn on his country, and he had chosen me. Or maybe he just wanted someone who already had security clearance and was expendable. I hoped it was the former.

Turning off the phone, I carefully slid the heavy bookcase away from the wall to expose the secret passage, when I was startled by the sound of the front door opening behind me. I wheeled around quickly while my mind searched for a way out of what was undoubtedly going to be an awkward situation.

For one, I didn't speak Arabic, but even without the language barrier, how was I supposed to explain to some Iraqi why there was a hidden staircase in the shop? And what if it wasn't just "some Iraqi"? Perhaps he was sent by Mickey, or even worse, a member of the Republican Guard, Saddam's security force. The door had been locked, hadn't it? I was pretty sure I had seen Jackson flip the deadbolt. Who would have a key? Or did they pick the lock? That ruled out a random shopper. Why hadn't I grabbed a gun before I came up the stairs?

My heart temporarily ceased its beating as I turned to face the noise.

Chapter 20

Sam smiled politely as he strolled swiftly across the shop, apparently unaware of the trepidation he had momentarily caused me. He grabbed the other end of the bookcase and began to pull. When he realized I wasn't helping, he looked across at me and frowned.

"What?"

I stood frozen in terror, staring at him with wide eyes. "You scared me to death," I panted. My heart restarted, and from my breathing, you would think I had just run a couple laps around the block.

He just shrugged. "Sorry."

"I thought you were one of Saddam's men."

He laughed. "Oh, don't worry. If one of them came after you, you would have been dead before you even knew they were here."

"Thanks. That makes me feel much better." He continued laughing, quite amused by my fear.

Replacing the bookshelf, we joined the others in the basement and found that everything in the small space—furniture, books, rugs, light fixtures—had been piled in the kitchen nook, as far from the door as possible. After Sam relayed the apparently hilarious account of how he had scared me upstairs, I changed the subject by updating them on my call with the president.

"He wants us to call back in fifteen minutes to check on the status of the satellite search," I concluded.

"We might as well wait down here until we hear more from him," Jackson declared. "Without the satellite image, we don't know where Mickey is headed."

"He went south," Sam announced.

"How do you know?"

"When I approached Madame in the garden, I told him that I had been sent back to the palace to inform him of the missing gold. I dropped a couple names of some people that I knew were aware of the location, and he apparently believed me. He started contacting military personnel stationed around the city and found out that a large truck drove out of town heading south this afternoon."

"How do we know it was Mickey?" Jackson asked skeptically.

"'Cause the truck was being driven by an 'Irishman'. Or at least that's what the guard thought."

"Good. Let him keep thinking that. We don't want the word 'American' coming anywhere near their lips."

"I wouldn't worry about that," Sam said with a confident smirk.

"Why not?" I asked.

"Well, when I heard the truck was headed south, I took the liberty of mentioning Kuwait. Madame already doesn't like them and jumped on the idea that the Kuwaitis hired someone to steal his gold. All his sycophantic buddies joined in, and by the time I left, they were even floating the idea that the man hired by the Kuwaitis was ex-IRA."

"Ha! Just because of his hair?" Tank seemed rather amused by their imagination.

"Pretty much," Sam nodded, equally amused.

"Alright, well, let's get going then." Jackson motioned toward the stairs. "We can call George on the way." Sam nodded his approval, and we climbed the stairs to the bookstore for the last time.

I helped Sam hide the secret passageway, and he once again felt the need to tease me about being scared by him. He was just getting to his favorite part, where he made the witty remark about the Republican Guard killing me, when Tank produced a small remote from his pocket.

"What's that?" I asked, eager to move on to a new topic.

"We're just gonna drop a little dirt on our room down there."

"You mean you're gonna set off a bomb."

He shrugged. "Actually several, but they're all small. Basically, a sink hole will appear behind the store, and the evidence of our presence will be buried."

And then he pressed the button. From below, I heard a small rumble, and for a few seconds the ground seemed unsteady. Then everything was quiet. It felt kind of like standing on a bridge when a large truck drove by.

"That's it?" I asked, expecting something much more dramatic.

"Yup. Doesn't take much. It's just like a dump truck dropping a load of dirt."

Before any of the neighbors decided to check on the cause of the minor earthquake, we piled into the van and headed south out of the city. Sam took over the sat phone duties and updated the President with the information he had received at the palace. From his embarrassed humility, it sounded as though George was pleased by his diversion of Saddam's focus to Kuwait and the IRA.

"We caught a break with the satellite search," Sam declared after hanging up the phone. "They have a good view of the truck leaving Baghdad and heading south toward the Persian Gulf." This was what we had expected, but it was nice to have confirmation that we were on the right track. Once outside the city, many of the roads left much to be desired, and we hoped it would be slow going for the large, heavy vehicle; that might give us a chance to catch him.

Subsequent to intercepting the truck, we had no concrete plan other than to "take care of the problem" as Jackson put it.

Chapter 21

I managed a few minutes of sleep as we sped through the desert, trying to reach Najaf ahead of Mickey. With all the excitement of the day, I hadn't realized how tired I was until I had the chance to relax in the van. Compared to my normal days spent sitting in a chair, this was about as much exercise as I could handle. It felt good to recharge, even if just briefly.

Between naps, I caught several updates from the President's satellite searches. Using this information, we were able to reasonably predict Mickey's escape route south to the Persian Gulf. A plan was developing to stop him, and Najaf had been chosen as the preferred point of interception. Sam was familiar with the area, and it was most likely in the truck's path of travel.

Determined to stop the fleeing "Irishman", Saddam had set up roadblocks in several cities south of Baghdad, so we decided that it would be best to intercept the truck out in the country, where we would be the least conspicuous.

"He'll probably be most vulnerable on this bridge northeast of Najaf," Sam declared, pointing to a map spread out across the bench seats in the back of the vehicle. "If I remember correctly, it's exposed on the north side, where he'll be coming from, but has decent cover on the south from a grouping of trees on a small rise."

"We could set up some sort of ambush," Tank offered over his shoulder from the driver's seat.

"What are the odds that he is actually going to cross that bridge?" Jackson asked.

"Well... I'd say maybe 50/50," Sam shrugged, "but it's the best chance we've got."

"What if we tag the truck somehow?" I offered. "Then we could follow him."

"Tag it with what?" Jackson asked.

"I dunno. You've got all kinds of gadgets in the back, don't you have any sort of GPS trackers or something?"

"Well, the sat phone does," Sam nodded, "but I don't know how we would attach it to the truck without him knowing."

"And then we wouldn't have our phone," Tank added. "It doesn't do us much good to track him if we can't talk to the President to find out where he's going."

"What if we marked the top of the truck with something visual?" Jackson suggested.

"What, like paint?" Tank asked.

"Sure. That would help them track it better with the satellite images."

"Could work," I said, "but again, how do we paint the truck?"

"Just tracking the truck is no good," Sam interjected. "What if he dumps it and switches to a different vehicle?" We all nodded slowly, lost in thought.

"Okay, so we make our move at the bridge," Jackson said decisively.

"That's great, but what's 'our move'?" I asked. I listened to the sounds of the road for several minutes, as everyone pondered the question.

"Well," Tank said finally, "we can't damage the truck. We'll need it to move the gold." This had not actually been discussed, although I had assumed that everyone wanted to recover the gold just as much as they wanted to stop Mickey. If it weren't for the gold, several other options would have been offered. We could just blow the truck up, or let him escape and track him down later. But we wanted that gold. Not only for the obvious monetary reasons, but also because taking it would be great revenge on Mickey.

"Okay," Sam nodded, "so we have to stop the truck somehow."

"How 'bout a roadblock?" Jackson offered. "We make it look like one of Saddam's, and then ambush him."

"Do you really think he's going to stop for Saddam's roadblocks?" I asked doubtfully. Surely Mickey was prepared for such a situation, wasn't he?

Sam waved his hand dismissively. "Plus he knows what we look like. We won't have time to disguise ourselves."

"So, what would he stop for?" Jackson asked.

The question triggered something in my mind, and an idea rose to the surface. It was a strange feeling that I had experienced only a few times before. It seemed like the idea had already been formed in my subconscious, and the finished product had only now been hurled violently into my consciousness.

If we were this concerned about the gold, wouldn't Mickey be at least as cautious? He might not stop for a roadblock, but he would certainly stop to save the truck and its contents. "Sam, how long is the bridge?" I blurted out.

"Uh... I'd say about three, four hundred feet. Something like that," he said, eying me curiously. He could tell I was onto something.

"And what's the support structure like underneath?"

"Steel beams with cement pillars, I think. Standard stuff. Why? What are you thinking?"

That's what I was hoping to hear. "I'm thinking we should blow up the bridge," I declared matter-of-factly. I watched as their faces changed from surprise to thoughtful consideration.

"Well, he would definitely stop if the bridge was out, but then he would be on the north side where there isn't any cover for us," Sam argued. "How are we going to set up an ambush from there?" I shook my head. They weren't catching on.

"No, I mean blow the bridge up while the truck is sitting on it."

Chapter 22

"How much time do we have?" I asked, wiping the sweat off my forehead with the back of my arm. This did no good, as my arm was already soaked, but I wasn't thinking clearly enough to realize it. My mind was focused on one thing, and one thing only.

"Maybe five, ten minutes. Don't know for sure. Just hurry the hell up, will you?" Jackson was getting annoyed. He wasn't the only one that was upset with me, but he was the worst at hiding it.

I stood on the narrow ledge, clutching the large pillar so tightly my hands were starting to hurt. *I guess that's what I get for running my big mouth, I* thought. When I had suggested blowing up part of the bridge, I hadn't imagined that I would be volunteered to climb underneath, a hundred feet above anything solid, and plant the dynamite. I had, of course, been too embarrassed to admit I didn't like heights and couldn't come up with any other excuse.

So, there I was.

The plan—my plan—was to wait until the truck drove onto the bridge. We would then proceed to blow a large hole in the road at the south end of the structure, causing the truck to stop and reverse. While the vehicle was momentarily motionless, we would blow the north end of the bridge, trapping the vehicle in the middle. Stranded on an island of cement above the Euphrates River, Mickey, and whatever small army he might be traveling with, would be sitting ducks.

This, of course, required precise timing and careful placement of the explosives—no small feat. We didn't want to completely destroy the bridge, just stop the truck. After taking possession of the cargo, we needed to be able to somehow return the truck to solid ground. That part of the plan was still a bit fuzzy, but I felt confident that we could figure something out.

Being the only engineer in the group, it was determined that I was the best man for the job. I protested initially, but Jackson reminded the others about my explosives work for the DOD back in college, and my fate was sealed. So now, ready to plummet to my death and paralyzed by fear, I couldn't seem to force myself to move away from the limited security of holding on to the pillar. I felt like a cat stuck in a tree.

The bridge was exactly how I had imagined it. The thick cement roadbed was supported by narrow steel joists running across underneath. These joists then attached to larger steel I-beams extending the long way down either side of the bridge. Cement pillars rising up out of the river suspended the whole thing in the air.

The column of cement I was now clinging to had a steel band around it in several places, providing me with a small ledge to stand on. This was only slightly comforting. I needed to move to the next pillar, about twenty feet away. Then I would have to climb up onto one of the iron cross braces running under the roadbed and duct tape the dynamite into place. Finally, I would attach the detonator and pray that I didn't blow myself up.

Somehow, it had all seemed so simple when I explained it to the guys in the safety of the van. But I had been envisioning someone else, someone more daring, completing the task. Now, I couldn't see any way to accomplish it successfully. Was this really the idea that the world's best think tank had decided on?

"It's just like the monkey bars when you were little—hand over hand," Tank tried to help.

"I never liked the monkey bars," I snapped. Did this guy seriously think that hanging from the bottom of an extremely tall bridge was 'just like the monkey bars'? Clearly the scale of the situation was quite different. But part of me knew he was right; that was exactly what I needed to do—hand over hand... and not die.

I checked the rope around my waist for the hundredth time. It was still tied tightly, but I fiddled with it for a while trying to stall. My eyes followed it back up to where it was connected to the side of the bridge above—still tied tightly there too. I was out of excuses. It was time to go for it. Maybe this would actually be a good thing. I had already survived a jump from an airplane. Facing my fears could be therapeutic. *Yeah, and dying will erase all of your fears*, I heard a voice say in the back of my head.

Gripping the pillar even tighter, I forced one shaky hand up to the steel beam. As my center of balance shifted away from the support and out over the chasm below, I panicked and jerked my hand back down to the cement. *Breathe*, I told myself. *You can do this.*

"Come on," Jackson moaned from land. "I'd like to make it home for the World Series in October."

That guy was really starting to piss me off. But then I noticed that, like on the plane, my anger seemed to calm my nerves a bit. It got my mind thinking about something else. Seizing the moment, I rallied up some courage, inhaled violently, and threw my hand into the air, grasping the hunk of metal tightly before I could chicken out again.

"Hallelujah!" Jackson called. "He moved." Sam and Tank joined him in a little mock applause.

With one hand now on the crossbar, I froze for a moment, unable to force my other one to release the pillar. I knew once I did, I would lose the security of standing; my feet would be dangling over the chasm below. I contemplated letting go of the crossbar again in order to return to the security of the pillar, but then told myself to grow a pair and suddenly, in one quick motion, I threw my other hand to the beam and released my feet from their platform.

As I swung out over the abyss, I tried to scream, but found my breath had left me. I could feel my heart pounding in my head as I began to panic. Every instinct told me to get back to the pillar, but my arms wouldn't move. I was afraid to stay where I was, but I was just as afraid to go anywhere else.

"Come on, Caleb," Jackson prodded. "Mickey could be here any minute. Move your ass." We didn't really know when Mickey would arrive, or even if he was for sure coming to this bridge, but everyone still felt that time was of the essence. I was beginning to think Jackson was purposely trying to make me mad. Perhaps he already understood what I was just learning about fear.

"I... I can't," I panted. My arms were starting to get sore, and I wondered how long I could hang on. *You used to be able to do this for over a minute*, I told myself. Back in high school, we'd had to do the flexed arm hang in gym class, and I had been one of the best at it. But I wasn't in nearly as good of shape anymore. And it probably didn't help that I was gripping the bar so tightly.

"Alright, hang on. I'm coming out there," Tank called, and I heard him scramble noisily down the rock ledge and onto the pillar behind me. From the sound of it, he wasn't nearly as hesitant as I had been.

"I'm gonna go call the President for an update," Sam declared. I didn't really care what he did, unless it involved getting me out from under that bridge.

"Okay," Tank said calmly, standing about a foot behind me. His gentle voice was back. "You can do this." I shook my head slightly, unable to speak. "Just go one step at a time," he prodded.

I wish I could take steps. Then I'd be on solid ground.

"Just look up at your target and imagine that the ground is only inches beneath your feet." I fixed my eyes on the next crossbar and tried to picture the ground just below me. However, I could still see the water in my peripheral vision.

"It's not working," I snapped.

"Okay, then close your eyes," he said soothingly. "You're on the school playground. Some kids are going down a slide. One of your friends calls to you from the merry-go-round." His low voice was very relaxing, and I actually felt myself starting to loosen up a bit. "That cute girl you like is at the other end of the monkey bars waiting for you," he continued. "You don't want to disappoint her. Why don't you swing across and see her?"

I took a few quick breaths, inhaled sharply, and reached for the next crossbar.

As my body swung forward, I made several hasty hand over hand motions, reaching my destination quickly. Feeling emboldened by my progress, and not wanting to give the fear time to take over, I immediately pulled myself up into a sitting position on top of one of the beams. I paused for a moment and breathed heavily, doing my best not to hyperventilate as I listened to Tank cheer for me and Jackson complain about how long it took.

I felt moderately more at ease in this position—sitting rather than hanging—and was able to slow my breathing enough to proceed with the task at hand. I removed my backpack and tried to focus on getting the dynamite taped to the underside of the bridge, but I was never able to completely remove the absence of land beneath me from my mind.

I stalled slightly as I attempted to tear the first piece of duct tape off. I didn't know if I could handle letting go with both hands, but there was no way to tear it with just one. I finally decided just to rip the tape with my teeth. The glue tasted awful, but I didn't care—at least I was safe. I found that by putting the tape on the dynamite first, I was able to attach them to the bridge one-handed, and I quickly developed a system of tearing and taping. It didn't take long to attach the explosive tubes, and I was ready to install the detonators.

Things were progressing quickly now, and it seemed as though my plan might work after all. I began to get excited about my design being put into practice, and the rush of adrenaline momentarily overshadowed my fear as I armed the explosives. Soon the backpack was slung back over my shoulders, and I was returning to the column below where I could stand once again.

I was feeling pretty proud of myself as I stopped to rest briefly before making the return trip to Tank, who was still waiting at the first pillar. Surely I would get some sort of hazard pay for all of this, wouldn't I? The trip had definitely gone far beyond anything I had envisioned during my quaint afternoon walk through The Rose Garden.

"Stop right there!" came a gruff voice from behind. All of my excitement melted away, and the goose bumps returned. As I slowly turned and looked back to solid ground, I saw Sam and Jackson, arms in the air, surrounded by guns.

Chapter 23

There were six of them dressed in typical Middle Eastern garb, and none looked friendly. All had Ak-47s either pointed at one of us or slung over their shoulder, and I could see several large pistols tucked into their belts. The biggest one had a long scar across his cheek that jumped the gap from his upper lip to his lower and made him look all the more menacing. He scowled at us as if we were the ones who had put the disfiguration there.

I clutched the pillar again, frozen by a new fear. Suddenly, plummeting to my death seemed like less of a pressing issue. In the midst of my panic, a thought crossed my mind. Wouldn't it be ironic if, after all the arguing in my head to convince myself that I wasn't going to fall, I was shot and ultimately tumbled to the riverbed after all?

A skinny guy with a bushy beard motioned for Tank and I to return to land. "Easier said than done", I wanted to say, but decided not to argue. I hesitated for a moment and considered my options. Blowing the bridge early would do no good and from my current position would most likely result in the addition of new holes to my own body. I couldn't stay where I was, and there was nowhere else to go but back toward the guns. This was the point where James Bond would have made some spectacular leap and swung to safety with the rope tied around his waist, taking out the bad guys in the process.

I really had no choice but to comply with their demands. With a deep breath, I looked up, pretended I was on the monkey bars again, and forced myself to make the return trip, hand over hand.

Despite the impending threat, I felt some small bit of relief by returning my altitude to zero. One imminent danger is better than two, I supposed. I untied my rope and listened as Sam argued with one of the gunmen in Arabic. I tried not to make eye contact with any of them, hoping that I wouldn't have to say anything.

While staring at the ground, I studied the men out of the corners of my eyes. I noticed one of them, tall and thin with a well-trimmed beard, stood back away from the other five. He was much calmer then his partners, with a pistol hanging loose at his side. The others had circled us and occasionally prodded us with a rifle barrel, just to make sure we understood that they were in control.

The man arguing with Sam was shorter and had a lazy eye, which made it difficult to determine who he was actually yelling at. Eventually, the tall, calm one stepped forward and took charge, interrupting the argument and pushing Lazy Eye a couple steps away from Sam.

"You are Americans, no?" he asked in heavily accented, but proper English. His pleasant tone, as if we were having a polite conversation, was a sharp contrast from the anger spewing out of the other men. I glanced nervously at Sam, who responded with rapid Arabic, apparently trying to convince them otherwise.

Tall Guy ignored Sam. "An American was killed in Baghdad this morning," he said, as if reading a headline out of the newspaper. "You were with him. Why?" I felt my body flinch slightly in surprise, and I hoped they had not noticed my reaction. No one responded. How could they possibly know that? Was he just guessing?

"You knew the dead American," he pressed.

"I don't know what you tossers are talking about," I said, trying to sound British, or Australian, or anything but American.

Bushy Beard laughed. "You talk like America." So much for that plan.

"Look, mate," Jackson joined in, "we're just journos on holiday from Melbourne. We were trying to get some pictures of a rare bird under the bridge there until you lobbed in and scared it off." Scarface responded with a sharp jab in Jackson's ribs from his rifle. The tall one, clearly in charge, shook his head and rattled off some more Arabic to his men. They began herding us down the road toward a dark blue panel van, shouting more directions. I couldn't understand anything they were saying, but the waving guns were pretty easy to interpret.

As we neared the back of the vehicle, the men stopped us and waited as the leader opened the rear doors and produced a large manila envelope. He removed several photographs from the package and tossed them on the gravel at our feet. Tank cautiously bent over and picked them up, watching for any hostile movements by our captors. We crowded around him as he flipped through twenty or so images of us entering and leaving the bookstore.

"So, do you still deny you know that man?"

"What makes you think he's dead?" Tank asked, attempting to continue the Australian accent, but sounding more like John Wayne.

"I have sources," Tall Guy replied with a confident smirk.

It occurred to me at this point that although we were being held at gun point, it didn't really feel like a ransom kidnapping. If they wanted to take us, we would be in the van already, wouldn't we? They obviously had control of the situation. And it clearly wasn't a robbery or we'd be lying dead on the side of the road already.

"What is it that you want from us?" I asked, sounding more confident than I felt.

The leader turned to me and smiled. He seemed amused by my attempt at being bold. "I have a business proposition," he answered. I shrugged and held up my hands to signify that we were ready to listen—not that we had any other choice. He approached Tank who was still holding the pictures and pointed at a shot of Mickey entering what we had thought was Evan's house with Sully.

"This man stole my gold."

Chapter 24

The back of the van was pretty cramped with the four of us crowded on a bench seat designed for three "average" adults, a group that Tank was clearly not a part of. They hadn't bothered tying us up, since we had no weapons, and they had plenty. And it wasn't as if we were going to suddenly jump out of the vehicle while it was flying across the desert at a ridiculous speed. I didn't know if they had much in the way of traffic laws in Iraq, but surely this guy was breaking any that did exist.

"Where are you taking us?" Jackson broke the silence after several minutes. We were traveling west on what they probably called a road, but seemed to me more like a loosely marked path. At times, I wasn't sure if we were even on a road at all. My suspicions were slightly confirmed by the fact that we had seen exactly zero other cars since leaving the bridge.

This was rather unexpected given the deafening explosion that had rocked the area shortly before our departure. Once we were in the van, Lazy Eye had searched my back pack and found the remote detonator for the dynamite under the bridge. He looked at it curiously and asked me something in Arabic before pushing the button. The blast had surprised his partners and Bushy Beard responded by firing his gun randomly in the direction of the bridge, a large section of which splashed into the river bed below. Once they realized what had happened, the van was quickly loaded, and we sped off through the desert.

My pathetic grasp of Middle Eastern geography gave me no information as to our possible destination; although I was pretty sure we were heading in the general direction of Saudi Arabia and Jordan, and away from the mountains in Iran where we had parachuted down several hours earlier.

"An Nukhayb," came the response from the leader, sitting in the front seat.

"Where?" I asked Sam, not familiar with the town.

"It's a small town near the border. It is where many Muslims pass through before entering Saudi Arabia on their way to Mecca."

"Oh," I nodded, as if this explained everything. So, we were close to Saudi Arabia. At least I had been right about that.

"I thought we were going to get the gold," I said to whomever wanted to listen up front. Before shoving us into the van, they had explained the supposed 'business proposition'. We would be held captive until such time as we helped them take the gold from Mickey. If we were successful in the endeavor, then we would be free to go. None of us believed it, but it was nice that the possibility was at least out there.

"We are," the leader replied. "The gold will be here in the morning." I glanced at Jackson on my left who seemed just as confused as I was. On the other side of him, Tank was just staring out the window, ostensibly oblivious to the conversation.

"And how do you know that?" I asked.

"Because your 'Mickey' is planning to sell it."

"To whom?"

"Ahmed Yassin."

"The Muslim Brotherhood?" Sam asked in surprise.

The leader shook his head. "Your information is outdated. He recently formed his own group. They call themselves "Hamas". He is planning to create a military branch and is looking for funding."

"How does buying gold help fund his endeavors?" I asked. Wasn't trading money for money kind of a wash?

"You don't see the big picture, do you?" Clearly I did not. "Your friend wants to get rid of that gold as quickly as possible. He will have a hard time getting it out of the region with Saddam after him. So, he will sell it for probably half its value. He still becomes incredibly wealthy, and Ahmed doubles his money."

Now I understood. It was a brilliant plan actually. Ahmed would certainly have more connections to smuggle the gold out of Iraq than Mickey would.

"And what is it that you plan to do with the gold?" Jackson asked.

The leader considered the question for a moment. "I suppose in many ways the same thing that Ahmed does."

"You're creating a military?" I asked.

He laughed. "No, you've already done that for me."

Suddenly Sam sat up a little straighter. "I knew I recognized you," he declared. "You're the one who helped start that mujahedeen training camp a couple years ago in Afghanistan, against the Soviets. Um... Osama, right?"

"Yes."

"I thought the war was over," Jackson declared.

"It is," he nodded, "but our organization is interested in expanding our efforts to include Islamist struggles in other areas as well."

"I see," Jackson nodded. "And what are you calling your organization?"

Osama considered the question, as if unsure of the answer. "Well, one of our main training camps during the war was simply called 'al qaeda'."

"The base," Sam translated.

"Correct. That name has just sort of stuck, and for now that's what we're going with."

"So, you call yourselves 'the base'?" Jackson said skeptically. "I gotta say, that seems kind of boring."

"The name is not important," Osama retorted. "Our work is what matters."

Jackson shrugged. "I dunno. I just can't see a group named 'the base' ever accomplishing much." He was clearly trying to push the man's buttons, and I wasn't sure if that was the best idea, given our current predicament.

"So, as I understand it," Sam jumped in, "your organization, as well as Ahmed Yassin's, both stem from the Muslim Brotherhood in Egypt. Why are you not working together?"

"Hamas will never be successful as long as they acknowledge those apostates that call themselves 'Shiites'," he said, spitting on the floor to emphasize his disgust. "Allah will not be on their side, and we will not associate with such people."

It was clear that we were upsetting an already angry man, and I decided to change the subject before he concluded that our assistance—and by extension, our existence—wasn't really that valuable. "So, what's your plan for getting the gold, and why do you need our help?"

He sat up a little, and in an instant the anger was gone, and his expression changed from religious zealot to schemer. He smiled mischievously and said, "You are going to be the distraction."

Chapter 25

Late in the night, we rolled quietly through the town of An Nukhayb. It was difficult to see much in the waning moonlight, but the town appeared to be very small. From what I could gather, it was just a collection of rundown buildings grouped together at the intersection of three major roads. It certainly seemed like a remote location that was out of the prying eyes of Saddam—perfect for a clandestine rendezvous.

I guessed the time to be around midnight as we parked in a junkyard on the south end of the town. The old rusty van blended right in with the twenty or so other vehicles sitting around waiting to be scrapped for parts, and it was hoped that no one would even be aware of our presence. Jackson nudged Tank to wake him up as the vehicle came to a rest, and we pried ourselves out of the van.

We briefly stretched our legs a bit before being herded into a broken down station wagon sitting on blocks. Even with the back seat missing, it was a tight fit for all four of us. We protested, and Sam argued unsuccessfully in Arabic that we could just as easily be locked in two different vehicles, giving us more space.

Our captors took turns standing guard throughout the night, and I tried to sleep, but found myself preoccupied with thoughts of home. I had been gone for two whole days, and Katie had probably filled my voicemail by now. I could already hear the messages playing when I got home.

"Hey, Caleb. I just got off the plane—waiting for my bags now. I hope work is going well today. I should be home in an hour or so. I'll call you then."

"Caleb, it's me. I just got your message. I was looking forward to dinner tonight. Oh well, maybe we'll do it tomorrow. I'm curious about this job opportunity."

"Hey, I just wanted to check in and see if you were back in town today. I was thinking about dinner tonight. Give me a call."

"Caleb, what's going on? It's been a day and a half now. I'm starting to worry. Call me."

"Just checking in again. I hope everything is okay."

"You know. You'd better hope something bad happened to you, because if you're just ignoring me, I might never speak to you again."

I was not looking forward to the conversation we would have when I got home, as I tried to explain that I had travelled the world as part of a super-secret group on request from the President. If that ridiculous story didn't sound like a lie, then I didn't know what would.

I shifted positions slightly, attempting to find a comfortable way to sleep in the driver's seat. The steering wheel was proving to be the biggest hindrance, as the tilt adjustment apparently no longer functioned. I sat up and tried to stretch my aching back a bit and noticed that Tank, sprawled across the back, was similarly having a restless night. Even with the back seat folded flat, Tank's head was cocked sideways against the wheel well, and his legs pressed up against the door behind me.

"Can't sleep?" I whispered, hoping not to wake Sam or Jackson.

"These cars weren't exactly made for someone my size," he responded with a chuckle.

I laughed, "I would think not. Apparently they didn't position the steering wheel for maximum sleeping comfort either."

"Oh well, it's just one night," he shrugged.

"And hopefully not our last," I added absentmindedly. I immediately regretted the statement.

I had just admitted that I was scared, and you weren't supposed to do that, were you? I was pretty sure it was one of those unspoken guy rules, like pretending it didn't hurt when you got beaned by a pitch in little league; secret agents are never afraid of dying. And this after my meltdown under the bridge? I busied myself with looking out the window at the junked cars around us, pretending to be on the lookout for danger.

About twenty feet in front of the car, and slightly off to the passenger side, I saw Bushy Beard, our guard for the next couple hours, sitting on a stack of tires. He had pieces of an AK-47 laid out on the ground beside his feet and appeared to be cleaning the gun. When I finally glanced back at Tank, he was smiling sympathetically.

"What's her name?" he asked.

I frowned. "Who?"

"You drifted off earlier and must have been dreaming. You said something about being sorry you didn't call, so I assumed you were talking to a girlfriend." *Great*, I thought. *Now I'm also afraid of my girlfriend. Real cool, Caleb.*

"Oh... uh, Katie," I said.

"Didn't get a chance to tell her you were leaving town?"

"No. She was on a business trip when I left. I managed to stop and leave her a voicemail saying I was going to be gone, but it's been two days now."

"She'll get over it."

"Yeah..." I said, but I wasn't convinced.

"The same thing happened with my wife the first couple times I took off."

I frowned in surprise. "You're married?"

Tank feigned offence. "Why shouldn't I be?"

"No, I didn't mean that..." I stammered. "I just..."

He laughed. "Don't worry about it. Sometimes I'm still amazed that I managed to trick her into thinking I'm a good guy."

"And she's okay with you disappearing all the time?"

"Well, it's not all the time, but I wouldn't say she's okay with it. I'd say... she tolerates it."

"Does she know what you do?"

"Not the details, but yes, essentially."

I nodded slowly, processing this new revelation.

"What's her name?" I said finally.

"Becky."

"Any kids?"

"A five-year-old boy and a two-year-old girl."

"So, it is possible to have a family and be on The Committee."

"Sure. Jackson just got engaged last month. We don't travel all the time. We do a lot of our work from home in fact. We all have secure video conference setups and do our meetings from the comfort of our own houses. In fact, some months I'm home more than my neighbor who works forty hours a week in a factory." Suddenly, The Committee was sounding like an even better job than I had originally thought. That was assuming we survived the next day of course.

"And don't worry," he added. "We're not generally in this kind of danger. These are sort of... unique circumstances."

"You mean because of Mickey?"

He nodded slowly and added mournfully, "And Sully." We both sat in silence for several minutes, remembering our fallen friend once again, and by extension, the perilous position our own lives currently occupied.

"Was he married?" I asked.

"Sully?"

I nodded.

Tank shook his head. "No, Sully was different. This job—saving the world and whatnot—this was his life. It wasn't that he didn't like women—he wasn't like *that*—he just..." Tank seemed to be searching for the words to explain. "His priorities were just different, I guess. He chose to make his life about more than just himself."

I thought I understood and nodded in affirmation. Tank yawned widely and slid his shoulders a few inches to the side, affording his head a bit more room. It was just a simple movement, but the whole car shifted suddenly. Jackson picked his head up and rolled to the other side, never opening his eyes.

"We'd better get some rest," Tank whispered. "It's gonna be a big day tomorrow." I nodded and turned to look out the window. Staring at the stars, I attempted to find the big dipper as my eyes drifted slowly shut.

Chapter 26

According to Osama's contacts, the meeting was supposed to take place in the town square at eight o'clock. By seven-thirty, we were herded into an alley down the street and stared down the barrels of two AKs while we waited. This would have made us nervous enough without the added stress of preparing to attempt a plan even more improbable than the bridge scheme. If we were going to get out alive, we would have to con Mickey and Osama simultaneously, all without scaring off Hamas.

We had been awake since just after six when the sunlight first pierced through the windows of the station wagon. Osama and his men seemed to be in a good mood. They had, no doubt, slept much better than us and were apparently excited about the prospect of recovering a large amount of gold. They chatted anxiously in Arabic as they consumed their breakfast, a large flat loaf of bread which they dipped in honey.

We watched hungrily until they had finally had their fill and tossed the remaining chunks of bread in our direction. Each of us ended up with just a small piece, but it had been enough to scare away the hunger pains of the morning. Now, more than an hour later, I could feel the rumbling beginning again.

"I don't understand," I said to Sam. "Mickey is just going to make the trade out in the open, in the middle of town?"

"The place is essentially deserted," he explained. "Dhu al-Hijjah, the month of the Hajj, has just ended. Most of the town's members work at the border crossing southwest of here and will surely be busy today." The Hajj, I remembered, was the annual pilgrimage to Mecca that all Muslims were supposed to accomplish at least once in their lifetime. Most people who lived in the area, however, probably made the trek more often, I figured.

"That's in Saudi Arabia somewhere, right?" I asked, thinking back to geography class in high school.

"Yup."

"But if everyone is on their way back from Mecca, won't they be coming right through the middle of town here?"

"Yes, but not until later in the morning. I assume that's why Mickey set the meeting for eight."

"Just remember," said Bushy Beard, waving a pistol in our faces, "if you try run, I shoot you."

"Yeah, I think we've got that concept down, thanks," Jackson snapped, pushing the gun away with the back of his hand. Bushy Beard stepped forward and, with a menacing glare, shoved the barrel of the gun into Jackson's cheek. Jackson just glared right back at him. Scarface stepped in and guided his partner away from the confrontation. They conversed briefly and it appeared he was scolding him in Arabic, and Bushy wasn't too happy about it.

"Cool it, man," Sam said to Jackson, "they're probably just as nervous about today as we are."

"Oh really?" Jackson retorted, and seemed ready to start in on Sam.

"Guys, knock it off," Tank interrupted. "Just stick to the plan and everything will be fine."

"Yes," Scarface added. "Stick to the plan. No funny businesses."

We were all a bit anxious and getting tired of having guns pointed at us, but things were not likely to get any better when we entered the square and interrupted the exchange out in the street. Perhaps it was the tension of the situation, or the fact that we were all quite fatigued, but the man's misquote seemed to get to us, and for several minutes we couldn't stop laughing.

"What is funny?" Scarface demanded.

We held up our hands in defense. "Nothing," I said.

Jackson tried to explain, "I think something got lost in translation." Scarface hesitated, unsure what to do. At the moment, they cared more about the gold then being disrespected. And they needed us if they wanted that gold. Luckily, his mind was made up for him.

Our laughter quickly disappeared when we heard a large vehicle rumble through town from the east and stop in the middle of the main intersection. One of our guards poked his head out of the alley to inspect the scene. He spoke briefly in Arabic with his partner, and we waited a few more minutes in hiding before being ushered out into the street.

"Here we go," Tank mumbled. He stepped to the side and allowed Sam to take the lead, who stepped forward with his hands behind his back. We strolled slowly down the street toward the meeting.

In the light of day, I was able to better assess our surroundings. The town square in An Nukhayb was basically just a large intersection where several major roads converged. From there, one could travel south to Saudi Arabia, north to Jordan, or northeast toward Baghdad. There were a number of plain looking buildings lining the street, many in need of serious repair. It reminded me of the projects back home in Pennsylvania and was a far cry from the architecture of Baghdad or even Najaf.

Surveying the scene before us, I saw a truck resembling a large U-Haul on the east side of the intersection and an old, white Chevy pickup on the west. Two men stood in the back of the pickup, and another three loitered nearby, all with AKs. Apparently that was the only rifle model available around here.

From a distance, I recognized Mickey standing in the middle of the open area, talking with who I assumed to be a member of Hamas. I could see five men on Mickey's side of the street, stationed at various points around the truck. I found it curious that the Hamas guards seemed to be protecting their leader, while Mickey's were protecting the truck, and I wondered if the former had been told what it was they were buying.

"Mickey!" Jackson called as we approached. "Thank God you're alive!"

Mickey spun around quickly, obviously caught off guard by our intrusion. He stood frozen for a second, not sure how to respond. All of the guns from both sides shifted their focus toward us, the unknown threat, and we halted our approach. I couldn't imagine a more vulnerable position—completely exposed and surrounded on three sides by nervous men with powerful weapons.

"We were worried after Sully got killed," Tank added. Cautiously, Mickey excused himself and moved in our direction, motioning for one of his nearby guards to follow. The man he was meeting with seemed unnerved by the interruption, and his eyes darted anxiously about the square, searching the many doorways and windows all around. The AKs in the pickup returned to the danger from across the square, and Mickey's men pivoted in response.

Our strategy, such that it was, had formed hastily in the station wagon earlier that morning. The extent of our plan, if you could even call it that, was to pretend like Mickey was still one of us. Hopefully he would believe that we hadn't figured it all out. Then, in the interest of keeping his treason a secret, he would help us get away from Osama's men. Of course, Mickey was a smart man—smart enough to know we weren't stupid.

Plan B, suggested by Jackson, was to run really fast and hope everyone was a bad shot. We had actually debated for several minutes at breakfast about which of the two plans had better odds of success.

"Look who we found." I nodded at Sam, our supposed prisoner, still standing with his head down and his hands seemingly bound behind his back. As the gap between us closed, Mickey's expression changed abruptly and he feigned recognition, as if he had only just now realized who we were.

"Boy, am I glad to see you guys," he grinned. "I didn't know what to do. I didn't think it was safe to go back to the bookstore." He was acting friendly, but I noticed his eyes searching us. He was probably looking for weapons, of which we had none thanks to our captors.

"Well, we're just glad to see that you're alive," I said.

Mickey hesitated as he eyed Sam. I could see the wheels in his head turning. *Do they know who he really is?* He decided to play along. "So... you found Evan, huh?"

"Yup," Tank nodded, "and you'll never guess what he tried to tell us."

Jackson jumped in, laughing. "He claims he's a Committee member."

"Really?" Mickey laughed nervously. "How ridiculous."

"Yeah, that's what we told him," Jackson agreed.

"How did you find me?" he asked suspiciously.

"We asked around and heard something about a meeting," Jackson said like it was no big deal. "You're not the only one with contacts over here."

Mickey stood for a moment, considering the situation. I got the impression he was trying to make a decision. I also noticed that he was keeping his distance. He clearly did not trust us. After a protracted silence, he inhaled sharply, indicating that a decision had been made.

"Look, guys, I've actually got some good news," he said finally, "but you'll have to give me a minute to finish up what I'm doing here."

"Well, actually," Jackson said, "we kind of need your help."

Mickey paused for a moment and flashed us a pained smile. "Sure thing, just give me a second." He turned halfway, then paused, and said almost over his shoulder, "I'm sorry for everything."

He spun on his heal and headed back toward the meeting. As he passed his guard, I saw Mickey's head bob slightly, as if he were nodding. In response, the man raised his Kalashnikov in our direction. He motioned with the barrel for us to step out of the street and onto the curb.

"Mickey, come on!" Tank called, but received no response.

Jackson took a step toward the square and called after him, "Alright, fine. Go get your thirty pieces of silver, but just so you know, you won't have time to enjoy it. They're all comin' for you, you son of a bitch." The guard shoved Jackson roughly in our direction, and he tripped on the curb falling sideways onto the hard sidewalk.

"You've been marked!" he yelled, as he pushed himself back up to a kneeling position. I reached down to help him stand and glanced over to see Mickey take a small black suitcase, about the size of a carry-on bag, from the Hamas man.

"What's the muzzle velocity of an AK?" Sam asked.

"Around 2300 feet per second," Tank answered.

Sam sighed. "Hmm... I don't think I can outrun that. So, what's plan C?" No one responded.

With directions in Arabic translated by Sam, we were instructed to line up next to the entrance of the town's post office. This side of the building was in the shade and the stone wall felt cool as I pushed my hands against it. I closed my eyes and tried to think of home. I pictured Katie sitting at the table as I served dinner. The smell of freshly cooked chicken drifted out from the kitchen. She smiled at me and seemed genuinely happy to be there.

The guard's boots thumped heavily on the concrete as he stepped up behind us. Jackson continued to berate Mickey from afar, but I wasn't listening anymore. It was all just background noise. The guard mumbled something in Arabic and Sam translated, "Any last words?" I inhaled deeply as every muscle in my body tensed up, and I braced for the inevitable impact.

Then the chaos started.

Chapter 27

The first grenade took out the pickup and presumably the two Hamas men in the back with it. Everyone was stunned momentarily as the quiet morning was rocked by the explosion. In the thunderous silence that followed, we spun around to see our potential executioner lying in a heap on the ground, a fresh hole in the back of his head. I stood frozen for a mere second that seemed to last forever, until time rapidly accelerated again as Tank hastily retrieved the gun lying under the body, and we ran to take cover in the alley we had emerged from minutes earlier.

As we dashed across the street, automatic gunfire rang out in the square. The noise seemed to come from everywhere, and I felt for sure we would all be mowed down at any moment. We could only hope that they kept each other occupied long enough for us to get to safety. I glanced toward the square just in time to see the man with the suitcase retrieve a pistol from the waistband at the back of his pants.

Logically assuming a double cross, he raised the weapon and, without hesitation, put a single bullet between Mickey's eyes. His head snapped back violently with the impact, and his body went limp. He fell heavily, collapsing in a heap of twisted limbs in the middle of the street.

Even in the midst of the terrifying scene around me, I was aware enough to notice that this didn't look anything like the stunt men in the movies; he seemed more like a rag doll, with his arms flopping around loosely in the air. In fact, the whole thing was on a scale far beyond anything I had experienced before. From the ear-splitting chatter of the guns to the speed with which it all took place, jumping out of an airplane didn't seem quite so frightening anymore.

One of Mickey's guards had been standing nearby, the only one not watching the truck, and he raised his weapon to fire at his boss's killer, but was struck in the neck by a bullet from across the square. He spun awkwardly to the ground, grasping his wound with one hand and spraying bullets wildly into the air with the other.

The three remaining Hamas guards retreated behind a small coffee shop while providing cover fire for their leader as he retrieved the suitcase and followed them. At least one shot from Mickey's men connected, clipping him in the leg as he fled across the street, but he managed to limp to safety with what I assumed was a good amount of cash.

Once the Hamas soldiers had retreated, the rain of bullets halted and two guards emerged cautiously from behind Mickey's truck to check on the man rolling on the ground and holding his neck. One stood watch as the other bent down to help stop the bleeding. We observed from the relative safety of the alley as a small round object flew off of a roof and rolled at their feet. The remaining guard at the truck shouted a warning, but he was too late. The second explosion spread the injured man and his two rescuers across the street in various places.

With the town square now nearly deserted, Osama's men emerged from various hiding places and converged on the truck. The lone guard made a valiant effort, taking cover behind the open door of the cab, and dropped two of his attackers before ultimately eating a bullet himself from behind. They finished the massacre by placing an insurance bullet through the forehead of each corpse lying in the street—including Mickey.

Realizing suddenly that now was as good a time as ever to resurrect Plan B, we turned to retreat down the alley, only to find Scarface and Bushy Beard still waiting for us. Our two captors directed us into the street once again and toward the truck where the others waited. We walked slowly, attempting to delay the inevitable.

"So, you're going to let us go now, right?" Jackson asked. He tried to sound confident in his declaration, but we all knew he didn't believe it—none of us did. Osama ignored the question and turned to the truck, where one of his men was opening the back. The latch was released and the door slid up, revealing a pallet stacked ten high with gold bars. The men all chattered excitedly when they saw it.

Osama barked orders, and the back was quickly reclosed and latched. Still talking rapidly and patting each other on the back, several of them climbed in the front, while Scarface stayed outside with his boss. His eyes narrowed as a wicked smile appeared on his face.

"Well, I guess this is it boys," Jackson declared. "It's been a pleasure working with you."

"This can't be it," I said, and then to our captors, "You said you would let us go." I thought I sounded a bit whiny, but I didn't much care.

"Just relax," Sam said.

"Relax?" I snapped. "What are you talking about?"

"Have a little faith."

"Look, no offense, Sam," Jackson joined in, "but in light of the extremists holding us at gunpoint, this is not the time to be getting religious."

"Stop talking," barked Scarface.

"Or what? You'll shoot us?" Jackson retorted. Scarface responded by stepping toward Jackson and pressing the gun barrel into his forehead.

"I hope you know who you're doing this for," Sam said, shifting the focus away from Jackson.

"Allahu Akbar," he responded, holding his gun up in the air.

Sam nodded toward Osama. "But what about your boss over there? You sure he feels the same way?"

"Osama is Allah's soldier."

"I'm sure he is," Sam replied sarcastically. "But where does he come from?"

"It just so happens," Osama replied, suddenly taking an interest in the conversation, "that I am a member of the bin Laden family, who are very close friends of the Saudi royal family."

"Yes, technically," Sam nodded, "but you are barely a member of the bin Laden family."

"My father is Muhammed Awad Bin Laden."

"No, I understand, but... I mean, your mother was basically just one of Muhammed's concubines, wasn't she?"

"She was his wife."

"Yeah, but they divorced right after you were born, so..."

I glanced at Tank with a quizzical look. What was Sam doing? Perhaps he was just stalling, but I didn't see how arguing with the man was going to improve our situation. The big guy shrugged, apparently as clueless as I was.

"What is your point?" Osama snapped, obviously agitated.

"It just seems strange, that's all," Sam said, raising his hands in resignation. "She marries this man with powerful connections, has a kid, and then divorces right away. Almost sounds more like a business deal to me."

"I've heard enough of this," Osama said with a dismissive wave of the hand. He turned to climb into the truck and rattled off some instructions in Arabic to Scarface.

"What'd he say?" Jackson asked Sam.

"You don't want to know."

Chapter 28

It's amazing what things go through your mind as you prepare to die. One would expect to feel scared, perhaps even a little panicked, but I found my impending execution to be merely an unfortunate event looming in the near future. Perhaps I was jaded by the near execution I had survived minutes earlier. Or maybe my mind was just choosing not to be aware of the gravity of what was coming.

I would like to say that I was calm because I knew that there was life after death, that my faith overcame my fear. But in reality, even though I believed in Heaven and that I was headed that way, it wasn't a concept that I could really grasp. It was like trying to take comfort in the fact that if the whole world was on fire, at least we could live in big domes underwater. I could no more comprehend the concept of life in Heaven than I could life in an underwater dome.

I knelt on the curb next to Jackson and stared at the ground in front of me, trying to ignore the gun barrel in front of us. So this was it. The end of the line was a little dump of a town in the middle of the desert. Well, at least it would be quick; a bullet to the brain should kill me nearly instantly. In some ways I suppose that was better than a prolonged fall toward a rocky river bed below.

I heard thunder in the distance and looked up into the sky. Suddenly, I found myself back on the little league field where I used to play as a kid. I was sitting on the bleachers next to my dad, watching the dark clouds roll gently toward us.

"Stupid storm," I muttered, kicking the bench in front of me. But I knew that I didn't really hate the storm, just the effects it would have. In fact, I actually enjoyed rain, and often looked forward to a good summer shower, but on this day, it was inconvenient and would mean the cancelling of our baseball game.

Dying was like the storm, I realized. I didn't mind death. I doubted I would even know I was dead once it had happened. What really bothered me was missing out on the rest of my life—marriage, kids, being a grumpy old man, sitting on the bleachers with my son when his baseball game was rained out. Being dead didn't bother me so much, but not being alive sounded terrible.

I heard praying, and suddenly I was back in the desolation of An Nukhayb again, kneeling in the dirt. To my left, Tank was quietly reciting The Lord's Prayer. Though I'd spoken those words a thousand times, they seemed to have new meaning now as I faced execution.

"Thy will be done, on Earth as it is in Heaven," Tank muttered. From somewhere in the back of my mind I heard, *if it is not possible for this cup to be taken away unless I drink it, may your will be done.*

"Give us this day our daily bread. And forgive us our trespasses, as we forgive those who trespass against us," he continued. And again the voice added, *Father, forgive them, for they know not what they do.*

I felt the first of the rain drops on the back of my neck and looked up toward the clouds as I joined in. "And lead us not into temptation, but deliver us from evil." Scarface was frowning at us and raised his rifle to Tank's head. "For Thine is the kingdom, the power, and the glory, forever..."

The crack of a rifle interrupted the conclusion.

Chapter 29

Time seemed to slow down as I watched him fall backwards, his arms extending out in front of him and flapping around, much the same way that Mickey's had a few minutes earlier. He collided with the ground in slow motion, sprawled out on his back, as his head bounced off the pavement with a loud crunch. A pool of blood began to form in the street almost instantaneously, and created a small river heading toward the storm drain. The echo of the rifle died away after a second, and the town became quiet again.

For a split second, we all stared in shock at Scarface's lifeless body. Then the wheels started turning, and we realized someone else was in the town. It certainly wasn't Osama's men who had just saved our lives, and I doubted the Hamas guys were anywhere near An Nukhayb anymore. There were only three of them, and one was injured; they would not be looking for a fight.

I spun quickly, searching for an explanation, and saw through the windows of the truck that Osama was just as perplexed. He shouted something, and one of his men jumped hesitantly out the passenger door. He began to cross the square in our direction with his rifle in hand, searching the buildings for any sign of danger. He had taken no more than ten steps before another shot exploded through the square. He dropped to his knees and lurched awkwardly, twisting to his right and nearly landing on Mickey's lifeless body. As he fell, a quick spray of bullets erupted into the dirt from his AK, and I ducked instinctively.

The men in the truck were all shouting excitedly now. They pointed at various buildings, each thinking they knew where the shots were coming from, but no one else ventured out of the cab. Osama barked some orders and the vehicle was quickly put in gear. As they sped out of town to the south, a barrage of bullets was released into the surrounding buildings from inside the truck.

Alone now in the square, I looked around at my comrades, and saw that we were all intact, physically anyway. We had been so surprised by the sudden turn of events, that we were still kneeling in the dirt and hadn't had the presence of mind to run for cover after the first shot.

"Amen, indeed," I said, surveying the damage. Altogether, twelve men had died that day, and yet the four of us had been shielded from the danger. Twice we were lined up for execution, and on both occasions our assassin was inexplicably shot in the head.

We stood cautiously, and I felt the instinct to run for cover, but then realized that it would do no good. As the military snipers say, "if you run, you'll just die tired." And besides, it seemed that, for now at least, this unknown marksman was on our side, though I didn't know why. He clearly wasn't after the gold, or he wouldn't have let the truck drive away. Were we going to be kidnapped yet again?

"What the hell just happened?" Jackson asked.

"I told you to have faith," Sam replied.

"So, what, did God shoot those bullets or something?" Jackson retorted skeptically.

"I didn't say that," Sam shot back, and then laughed. "But you've got to admit, the timing was appropriate."

We searched the windows and doorways of the buildings overlooking the square, attempting to locate our savior, when we heard a door open behind us. Spinning around, we watched as Sully emerged from the shadows of the building and stepped out into the sunlit street.

Chapter 30

y first instinct at seeing Sully was one of dread. Was I dreaming? I'd had realistic dreams before, but surely this was not a dream, was it? Or worse, was I dead? Had I been executed? Perhaps I had been hit in the crossfire without realizing it.

No, I decided, I wasn't dreaming, and I definitely was not dead. I was fairly confident that this was not heaven, and although my current situation was certainly less than desirable, it didn't seem terrible enough to be hell either. So then, what was I seeing?

Perhaps it was a hallucination, brought on by the heat and stress. Maybe it was just someone who looked sort of like Sully, and my mind was playing tricks on me. I squinted at the figure as he strolled calmly across the street toward us with a large rifle slung over his shoulder.

"Sully!" Jackson exclaimed. Were we having the same hallucination?

"You're supposed to be dead," Tank added.

"Yeah, well, clearly I'm not," Sully laughed as he approached the group. Was it a ghost? I wasn't sure that I really believed in ghosts. Maybe a guardian angel...?

We all hung back slightly, unsure of what to think. Except Sam. With a big grin, and showing no hesitation at all, he stepped forward and greeted Sully with a warm hand shake and a one-armed guy hug.

"It's about time you got here," Sam declared. "I was beginning to worry."

"Wait. You knew he was alive?" I asked incredulously.

Sam shrugged and glanced at the ground, slightly embarrassed. "Well... yes."

"Russo helped me set the whole thing up," Sully explained.

I shook my head. "I don't understand."

"I knew there was a traitor in the group," he explained. "Sam and I worked together on a few projects back in the 70s, so when Mickey showed me the picture he'd received from his KGB contact, I knew something was up. I got in touch with Sam and asked him for help in finding the root of the problem. I figured since it was his picture being presented as the enemy, he was probably the one person I could trust."

"We didn't know if it was Mickey," Sam added. "He could have been given bad intel or something. Who knows? So, we had to find out for sure."

"But the blood and the fire at the house..." Jackson pressed.

"Well, the blood was fake. Mickey really did shoot me, but I was wearing a vest—still hurts like a mother, by the way." He rubbed his chest and grimaced. "And when Sam carried me upstairs, I simply walked out the back door before he started the fire."

"But you had no pulse," I argued. "We checked." As soon as the words left my lips, I knew the answer.

"Sam checked," Tank said, almost to himself.

"But what about the letters I found at Castro's place from Evan? Mickey didn't plant those, did he?" I asked.

"Oh, no. Evan is real," Sam confirmed. "It's just the image that was fake."

"Neither us nor the KGB know what he looks like though," Sully added.

"I'm not so sure about that anymore," Sam said.

"Why not?"

"Well, those men you shot, they were working with Osama Bin Laden."

"Bin Laden... you mean from the Saudi family?"

Sam laughed. "Well, technically. You remember him; he was the one that led the mujahedeen against the Soviets in Afghanistan."

"What was he doing here?" Sully frowned. "Is he in with Hamas now?"

"No. He was just after the gold. But, I've had my suspicions about him for a while. His mother's strange marriage, birth, and divorce always seemed suspicious to me, like he was purposely being bred into an influential family or something."

"So, what are you saying?"

"I'm just saying it's possible. We know Adolf was in Cuba at the time, helping Castro take control."

"You're saying Osama is Adolf Hitler's son?" Jackson said doubtfully.

"No, not Adolf's. Eva's."

Sully didn't seem to be buying it. "And Mohammed Bin Laden was some sort of hired stud?"

Sam shrugged. "Something like that." He looked around and saw our skepticism. "I dunno. Maybe it's not true. I'm just thinking out loud. It sure seemed peculiar how he randomly showed up and grabbed us though. He asked us questions about you, Sully, and he knew we were in Baghdad. But the thing that really got me thinking in the first place was when he said that Mickey stole 'his' gold."

Sully was tired of arguing. "I dunno, maybe. We'll put it in the report for George and look into it later."

"What I don't understand though," I said, changing the subject, "is why you didn't rejoin the group after you knew Mickey was the traitor."

"Well, for one, I didn't know if Mickey was working alone, and two, if Mickey thought I was dead, I was free to move about and keep an eye on him."

"And it's a good thing you did," Jackson added, "or we'd be in sad shape right now."

"Yes, but enough talk," Sully smiled. "We need to get the gold out of here."

"What gold?" I asked.

"You mean the stuff in the back of the truck that Osama just drove off in?" Jackson added.

Sully laughed dismissively. "Ah, that was nothing. Maybe a few million bucks at most."

"What are you talking about?" Tank argued. "I bet there were a thousand bars in that truck, at a couple hundred grand apiece."

"Ah, so his plan worked."

"What plan?"

"Well, as you know, I've been watching Mickey over the last day or so." We all nodded. "Well, last night, he stopped a few miles north of town and unloaded the gold from that truck, replacing it with scrap metal. He loaded up the pallets with chunks of steel and then stacked gold bars in the front so that it looked like there was a whole pile."

"He was trying to cheat Hamas?" Jackson exclaimed.

"Yup. Pretty much."

I was smiling now too. "You know where the rest of the gold is, don't you?"

He nodded. "I do indeed. And since all of Mickey's guys are gone," he motioned to the bodies littering the ground all around us, "I'm the only one who does."

"Well, then let's go get it."

We walked quickly out of town to the north, on the lookout for any danger, although we were pretty sure that everyone had probably cut their losses and run. It had been a bloody morning in the peaceful little town, and the travelers would be in for a surprise on their way home from Mecca.

We searched through Mickey's clothing to remove anything that could identify him as an American before leaving, but left the other bodies untouched, aside from confiscating a few weapons. The gun shot to Mickey's head from point blank range had left him badly disfigured, and we were confident that no one would be able to identify him, let alone connect him back to us.

An hour, and several miles, later, we found a rusty old truck hidden among some trees off of the road. It was concealed well, so that a passing motorist would not notice its presence unless he was looking for it. Even with Sully's knowledge of its location, we still nearly walked right by it.

It appeared to be an old delivery truck of some sort and had two heavy doors in the back. Using the butt of a gun and Tank's muscles, we managed to break the padlock and swung open the doors. Everyone gasped at the pile of gold inside. It was much more impressive than the truck Osama had taken. I counted five stacks, each fifteen bars high.

"How much is it?" I asked, still staring.

"Well, I don't know today's exchange rates," Sully was doing the math in his head, "but I'd say around three quarters of a billion." Hearing the number out loud suddenly made us nervous, and Jackson began to quickly shut the door.

"Let's get going then," he said, glancing back at the road. Even in such an isolated location, it was impossible to feel comfortable with that much money out in the open.

"What's the plan?" I asked.

"I've got a contact in Arar, just across the border into Saudi Arabia," Sully said. "We can get some grub there and make arrangements for transport."

Grub, as in food. Sounded good to me.

Chapter 31

"I have a question," I offered, as we navigated a side road around An Nukhayb to avoid the obstacles in the town square.

"Shoot," Sully replied.

"Well, Mickey was meeting with Hamas to sell them the gold."

"Right."

"And that was because he didn't want to try to get it out of the country."

"Yeah."

"And now we're gonna try to take the gold out of the country?"

"What's your point?" He didn't seem to be catching on.

"What do we have that Mickey didn't?"

"One of Saddam's... uh, what's your position again, Russo?"

Sam considered the question. "Well, it's sort of vague... the translation would roughly be 'Director of Operations', though which operations I direct varies somewhat from day to day. Saddam is very paranoid, and doesn't like anyone having too much control. By moving people around a lot, no one is ever really sure who is in charge of what. It seems to be a very effective tactic."

"Sounds like it would make for an inefficient government," I observed.

"What government isn't?" Jackson joked.

Sam nodded, "Well, Saddam is not real concerned with governmental efficiency. That's one of the great things about being a dictator; you don't have to run for reelection."

"There are plenty of great things about being a dictator," Tank added. "But very few if you are the one living under a dictatorship."

"Indeed," Sam agreed.

We continued to discuss the various benefits of different governmental systems and before long, the Saudi Arabian border came into view. With its large arches extending out of the desert over the highway, it looked out of place, like a toll booth in the middle of nowhere.

"Alright, this is it, gentlemen," Tank announced.

"Everyone just act bored," Sam said. "Bored people never seem suspicious."

"But people acting bored do," Jackson countered.

"Well," Sully interjected, "then I guess we'll have to do a good job of acting."

"Don't worry, it'll be easy," Sam assured us. "They'll be more focused on all the people coming back into Iraq from the Hajj."

As we approached the crossing, it quickly became clear that Sam was right. Across the median, a long line of cars waited to leave Saudi Arabia, but our side of the street was deserted. The truck rolled to a stop as we pulled under the archway and waited nervously for a border official to check us through. But none came. I could see five uniformed men working the other side of the road, clearing several cars at a time. They apparently hadn't noticed our arrival.

"Maybe we should just drive through?" Jackson suggested.

"No," Sam replied. "That would definitely warrant an inspection. We're trying to avoid that, remember? I'll take care of it." He climbed out of the truck and shouted something in Arabic at the nearest border guard. The man flashed an annoyed look in our direction, waved a family in a large Buick through the checkpoint, and jogged over to Sam. We could hear their conversation through the door that Sam had left open, and Sully translated quietly for us.

"Busy today," Sam observed.

"Everyone is headed home from Mecca," the guard responded. "What's your business in Saudi Arabia?"

"None," Sam shook his head. "Just passing through on our way to Jerusalem."

The man glanced questioningly at us in the truck. "Americans?"

"Tourists," Sam explained with disgust. An angry motorist honked his horn impatiently on the other side of the road, and the guard hesitated for a moment, obviously trying to make a decision.

"You're just driving straight through to Jordan?" he asked.

"Yes, sir. Hope to be there by sundown."

"And what's in the back?"

"Their luggage. You know how Americans are. They can't leave home without their luxuries."

The guard laughed. "Alright, go ahead." He waved his hand, indicating we were clear to pass, and returned to the backlog of travelers waiting across the median.

Sam climbed back into the truck. "See?" he said. "Nothing to it."

Chapter 32

'Driving straight through' wasn't entirely false. Apart from a brief stop in Arar, we were driving straight through Saudi Arabia, just not in the direction Sam had indicated. Instead of traveling northwest out of Arar to the Jordan border, and ultimately arriving in Jerusalem, we planned to head southwest toward the Red Sea.

It was about dinner time when we arrived in Arar, and we found Sully's contact, introduced as 'Joe', at home in his small apartment. He was surprised to see us at first, but after the initial shock, he became very friendly and chatted in rapid broken, but understandable, English. He seemed very interested in American culture and was eager to impress his visitors. When Sully introduced Jackson, Joe's eyes lit up.

"Like Michael," he exclaimed.

"What?"

Joe then burst into an off-key chorus of Thriller and attempted to moonwalk across the living room. Jackson found it impossible not to laugh as he explained that "Jackson" was actually a very popular surname and that he was in no way related to the pop singer. Joe seemed disappointed and informed us that Michael was "the best". Sully tried to shift gears and began to explain to him the events of the past day, downplaying the incident in An Nukhayb and the amount of gold we had recovered.

"We acquired a few bars of gold from Saddam," he explained.

"Really?" Joe exclaimed. "How big of numbers?"

Sully shrugged, "Enough that we'll leave one for you when we go."

Joe was very excited about the prospect of having something that had been stolen from Saddam, and Sully explained that Joe was born and raised in Iraq. A former member of the military, he had defected after receiving a death sentence for refusing to follow orders relating to a chemical attack on an

Iraqi city. He despised his former leader and talked at great length about the "monster who kills own people".

"We're going to need a few things," Sully interjected after several minutes of trash talk about President Hussein.

"Of course," Joe nodded. "Any what you need."

"Do you happen to have a satellite phone?"

"Umm... no, just the usual one. But you are welcome to ring it. It is in the kitchen."

"It'll have to do," Sully replied grimly. "Jackson, go call Judy and leave a message for George. Tell him we're gonna need a lift from the Navy." Jackson disappeared down the hallway. I wanted to ask who Judy was and why we couldn't call George directly, but I figured it would be best to wait until Joe wasn't around. At this point, I didn't really trust anyone, even if he was Sully's friend.

"And grab some food on your way back," Tank called after him.

"There is fruits in 'frigerator," Joe added, "and I think bread in the panty."

Tank smiled. "I haven't had panty bread for a while. That sounds good." We all laughed, and Joe frowned, obviously not getting it. Sully just shook his head and explained that it was an 'inside joke'.

Joe nodded and pretended to understand, but I could tell that he still thought we were making fun of him. "So, your plan is what?" he asked.

"I thought we'd just head down through Tabuk to the sea and hopefully hitch a ride from the Navy," Sully explained.

"I have a man friend in Duba," Joe said. Tank started to make another joke, but Sully quickly cut him off.

"Can we trust him?"

"Yes. He is very trustworthied. His name is called Khalid."

"Hmmm..." Sully considered as Jackson returned from the kitchen with a plate of various fruits, nuts, and breads. "Well, it would be helpful to pick up some supplies at the coast. Do you think you can get a hold of him this evening?" Jackson passed around the plate. I took a large apple and some sort of hard roll.

"You are soon to leave?" Joe asked with surprise.

"Yes, there may be people looking for us," Sully explained.

Joe nodded enthusiastically. "Try I will."

I took a big bite out of the apple and interjected as seriously as I could, "Do or do not. There is no try."

Tank and Jackson cackled loudly and I saw the beginnings of a smile on Sully's face as he shook his head.

"I'm working with children," he complained to our host who was once again out of the loop. "See if you can get your friend to meet us in Duba later tonight. Let him know that he will be compensated in the same manner as you."

Joe excused himself to make the call while we devoured his food and quoted more Star Wars lines.

Chapter 33

It was relatively cool as the day winded down. The sun was nearing the horizon, and I noticed a light fog settling in. The warmth of the ground prevented it from touching all the way down, however, and the moisture floated above us like a high ceiling. Any building taller than about fifteen or twenty feet disappeared gently into the cloudy mist.

We quickly finished loading our stuff into the truck, hoping to complete the task before dark. Although we had been successful in recovering the gold, the moment was bitter sweet, as the group was also feeling the effects of losing a friend. It wasn't

Mickey's death that produced the void as much as it was his disloyalty. The moment we first saw the four leaf clover smeared in blood, a gaping hole had formed in the committee.

I was less upset than the others though, partly due to the short amount of time I had known Mickey, and partly due to the fact that his departure left a spot for me to easily slide into. Sully had been right in Mexico when he said I was already on the committee. I couldn't see any possible way that I would be able to return to my mundane job at McHenry Steel after the adventure I'd just had.

Aside from the obvious brushes with death, the only negative for me had been missing dinner with Katie. She had been away for nearly a week, and I had already been anxious to see her. Now it had been two more days, though it felt like longer, and I wasn't sure how mad she would be when I returned. But then there was the money. I now had the ability to by a ring and maybe even a down payment on a small house. Surely the mysterious absence would be forgiven when I told her about the money.

"Alright, let's get going," Jackson directed as the sun began to dip below the horizon. Tank swung one of the big doors shut on the back of the truck, and as he moved toward the other, Sully stopped him and reached in to grab a gold bar. He slipped it into his worn backpack and hefted it up over his shoulder. He was smiling gently and his eyes appeared moist. I knew immediately something was up.

"Well, gentlemen, it was a pleasure serving with you. But Jackson's right, it's time for you to leave," he declared. I didn't understand. Wasn't he coming with us? In my mind I was questioning him, but I remained silent because the others didn't argue with him.

Sully gave one more pained smile and a slight nod in my direction, then turned and strolled casually up the hill to the east with the fading sun on his back. I stood in silence, watching him depart until he finally disappeared from sight into the fog.

I turned back to the truck and saw Tank locking the rear doors. Jackson and Sam were climbing in the cab, and I hurried to join them. The diesel engine roared loudly as we began the long drive west toward the Red Sea.

"So, he's not coming back, is he?" I broke the silence once we were outside of the city.

"He's been on the committee a long time," Jackson said. "It was his time. He'll be missed, but these things happen sometimes."

"You make it sound like he died."

"He did," Tank said somberly. "Mickey double-crossed us and shot him in a basement in Baghdad."

"That's right," Sam said. "I dragged his body upstairs and burned it myself."

"Isn't that right?" Jackson prompted.

I nodded slowly. "Yeah, I guess that's pretty much how I remember it."

"Make sure you do."

So, Sully was retiring. The fake death gave him an easy way to disappear, and the Nazis had unknowingly supplied his pension in the form of a swastika laden bar of gold. I suppose it wasn't a bad way to end things.

The long drive across Saudi Arabia finally afforded us a chance to relax. As far as we could figure out, no one was after us anymore.

"Saddam is focused on Kuwait, thanks to Sam," Jackson declared.

Sam shrugged. "Now that we're out of Iraq, we're pretty much safe from him anyway."

"Well, either way it was good work," Jackson said with a nod. "And I don't think Hamas has any idea who we are."

Tank chuckled, "They certainly seemed to be caught off guard by the incident. I'm not sure that they even realized there was a third party involved. The main guy seemed to think that Mickey was turning on them."

"I don't think any of Mickey's guys made it out," Sam said, recalling the events of the morning.

"Not that I saw," Jackson agreed, "but even if they did, I doubt Mickey told them his true identity. They were just hired thugs. My guess is they didn't know who he was or what they were selling."

That left only one person.

"What about Osama and 'The Base' or whatever he's calling it?" I offered.

"Well," Sam said, "he thinks that he got away with all the gold, right?"

"Assuming he doesn't know how much gold Mickey took," Jackson pointed out. "You were the one that said the gold might have been his in the first place."

"Good point," I nodded my agreement.

"But he lost quite a few men as well," Sam argued. "I don't know that he's gonna be real anxious to come after us again."

"Maybe not," Jackson conceded, "but just in case, we should stay on our guard until we get out of here." Everyone concurred, though we all believed the worst was over.

And we couldn't help feeling somewhat invincible too. So many people had died that morning in the firefight, and yet the worst any of us needed was a change of shorts. It had been the single most exciting, and terrifying, day of my entire life.

I began to feel the effects of my easing nerves, and I quickly began to doze. I tried to fight it at first, but gave in after a few minutes. Just a short nap would be fine. Then I could stay alert while someone else slept.

As I faded into dreamland, I heard Jackson and Sam discussing the plan for our arrival in Duba.

Chapter 34

I awoke slowly as the car accelerated around a corner. Confused, I picked my head up and looked around, attempting to get my bearings. It was very dark outside, but we appeared to be driving through a city, because I could see several store fronts illuminated by the street lights.

"Where are we?" I asked.

"Duba, Saudi Arabia," Jackson replied.

"Duba... already? How long was I out?"

"About six hours. Feel better?"

"I don't know yet," I groaned. My neck was stiff from the strange position I had been laying in. "I didn't mean to sleep that long."

"It's good for you," Sam said. "Short naps always make me more tired." I nodded slowly as I rubbed my neck, not necessarily in agreement, but mostly just because I didn't feel like arguing.

"So, no incidents I assume then?" I asked.

"Other than a car chase through the desert and another shoot out with Osama? No, no incidents," Jackson said.

"What?" I exclaimed.

Tank laughed, "You slept right through the whole thing."

I shook my head in confusion. "Wait a minute. I know I'm a heavy sleeper, but there's no way..." I was interrupted by laughter from the rest of the group.

"There was no shoot out," Sam offered. "We just drove through the boring ass desert for six hours. I haven't been this bored since visiting the in-laws for Thanksgiving last year."

"And you would prefer to be shot?" I asked.

"Well, not shot... but maybe shot at," he replied. "At least it would give me something to do."

"Careful what you wish for," Jackson said. "We've still got to get a boat and try to contact the ship. It's getting pretty late. I hope we don't have to wait until morning."

Great, another night in the desert. That's just what I needed.

"Let's hope Khalid is still down at the docks," Tank said.

"And that he's as trustworthy as Joe says," I added.

"Hey, if Sully says he's okay, then he's okay," Jackson retorted, apparently offended by my implication.

"I know, I know," I said, holding my hands up in defense, "but Sully's not around anymore. We're on our own now, remember?" My reminder seemed to briefly sadden everyone again, as we recalled the ups and downs of Sully dying, resurrecting, and then ascending into the mist, probably leaving us forever.

"Well, either way," Jackson said finally, bringing everyone back to consciousness, "it's our only option at this point." He drove through a stop sign and turned off of the road into a small parking lot along the shore.

It was very dark now in the middle of the night. Scanning the horizon, I saw a loan light bobbing out over the water. It was a bit late to be fishing, so I assumed it was probably a house boat. We scanned the area for any sign of Khalid, but the beach seemed to be deserted. My nerves at attention once again, we piled out of the truck and stretched for a moment in the parking lot. I was still trying to work the kink out of my neck as we debated what to do next.

"I thought this guy was going to be waiting for us," Sam compained.

"Well, it is pretty late..." Tank attempted to explain.

"He's here," Jackson said confidently. "There's no way he would pass up this kind of money."

It was clear that he was not in the parking lot. Our truck was the only vehicle present, and the cement pillars lining the grass on three sides were definitely not large enough to conceal a person. Outside of the pillars, however, there was a myriad of places for someone to hide.

The parking lot sat at the end of a T-intersection, where the main road into town connected with another running parallel to the water. There were any number of dark windows in the buildings facing the sea. Several cars sat abandoned along the curb. I could make out the dark outline of at least ten boats floating calmly, tethered to their docks for the night.

"So, what? We just wait then?" Sam asked skeptically. Jackson shrugged, and we resumed our scan of the area. No one wanted to venture too far from the truck—partly for our own safety, and partly for the safety of our treasure. Of course, safety was relative.

We were just about as exposed as we could be in our current position. All of our hope had been placed on the theory that no one knew where we were, and that the mysterious "Khalid" could be trusted. It seemed a bit foolish to go into this with no backup plan, and I wondered if perhaps fatigue was starting to affect the group's judgment. I considered expressing my concerns to the others when the lights on one of the parked cars flashed twice and went dark again.

"Did you see that?" I asked.

"What?" Jackson asked, spinning around toward the street.

"That car's lights flashed," Tank declared.

"Do you think that could be him?" Sam's voice seemed to have a bit of hope in it again.

"Your guess is as good as mine," Tank replied.

"There's one way to find out," Jackson said, returning to the truck. He reached in the open driver's window and flicked the lights on and back off again. I watched the car carefully, ready to run if needed. I had been a swimmer in high school, and I debated how far I'd be able to make it in the sea if I had to.

Lights flashed in the street once again, and the car's engine roared to life. We watched, breathless, as the mysterious vehicle rolled slowly past us through the intersection. It was a forest green sedan, and the dark figure in the driver's seat gave the appearance of a shadow driving the car.

"Get in," Jackson commanded. "It's him." We piled back into the truck and pursued the vehicle.

We followed him for several minutes through the dark, deserted streets of Duba and exited the city to the south on a road that roughly followed the shoreline. I began to worry that he was leading us out to a remote location for an ambush, when we finally came to a stop next to an isolated shed on the beach about two miles outside of town. The car's lights went out, but Jackson kept the truck running, ready to bolt if needed.

Our headlights illuminated the short, stocky man in thick glasses as he extricated himself from the car and glanced around nervously before looking our way and nodding toward the small building. Wearing khaki pants and a dark blue button up shirt, he carried a thick book and reminded me of a librarian.

"Sam," Jackson ordered, "take Caleb and go inside. Tank and I will keep an eye out for trouble."

"Why me?" I blurted out.

"If it's a trap, they'll be after the gold," Jackson explained impatiently. "That makes the truck the more dangerous place. If you'd rather stay out here, then be my guest." It was a good point.

Sam and I jogged cautiously to the open door of the shed and stepped inside. A single bulb hung from a rafter in the center of the room, only slightly lighting what appeared to be a small boat house, with fishing poles, ropes, and life jackets strewn throughout the room. To our left, makeshift racks stuck out from the wall, holding several row boats.

The man, whom I assumed was Khalid, was taking a padlock off the back door as we entered, and he nodded toward the boats. They were a bit small to be rowing around in the sea with at night, but just a few minutes prior I had contemplated a swimming escape, so boats sounded like a great idea.

I helped Sam hoist one of them down to the floor. To my surprise, it appeared to be in decent shape and was fairly clean on the inside. They had fiberglass hulls with two wood slats inside for sitting and were essentially the same as the ones fishermen used back home in Iowa. I grabbed two paddles from a stack in the corner and tossed them in.

Once the back door was opened, Khalid poked his head out and again looked around uneasily. Apparently satisfied that we were alone, he returned to the room and spoke briefly in Arabic with Sam, occasionally glancing anxiously in my direction. He looked very uneasy and alternated between scratching his head and adjusting his glasses as he spoke.

Sam produced a gold bar from a cargo pocket on his pants and Kahlid quickly slipped it into his book, which was actually a hollow case in disguise. Their business concluded, he mumbled some sort of valediction in Arabic while nodding in my general direction and exited the structure with his newfound wealth. After waving out the door to let Jackson and Tank know everything was okay, Sam returned to assist me.

"We can take anything we need," he said.

"How many boats do we want?" I asked.

Sam considered for a moment. "Well... there's four of us, so we'll need two boats, plus another one for our... cargo."

"Okay, then we need some rope too. We'll have to tow the cargo." I retrieved several rolled up ropes hanging on nails in the wall, as Jackson and Tank entered through the back door.

"We stashed the truck in back," Jackson informed us, "but let's not stick around too long."

"Agreed," Sam nodded. "Grab one of these boats and load up the gold. Try to keep it out of sight though." Tank and Jackson pulled another boat from the rack and maneuvered it out the door. As they emerged into the starlight, something caught my eye on a shelf nearby.

"Here," I said, tossing a folded up tarp over Jackson's shoulder. It landed in the boat with a thud. "Cover the 'cargo' with this."

"Good thinking," Jackson said, and they disappeared out of the building.

Sam and I finished loading up the other two boats with oars, life jackets, rope, a net, and even a filet knife. We didn't know what we would need, or how long we would be out there, so I wanted to be prepared. I searched the corners of the shed and found an old tool box, from which I retrieved a pair of wire cutters and a buck knife. I turned back to the boats to see Sam hoisting a scuba tank into one of the vessels.

"You really think we'll need that?" I inquired.

"Hey, you never know," he replied with a shrug. "It could come in handy."

"I guess."

Jackson and Tank returned to the shed.

"We're gonna need a fourth boat," Jackson declared.

"Why?" Sam asked.

"Too much gold," Tank explained.

I laughed. "Well, that's a good problem to have." Everyone agreed.

We finished carrying the boats out to the shore and loaded the rest of the gold. It took a bit of maneuvering and jostling to get all the boats into the water and tied together correctly, but we made it work while staying fairly dry. With one final glance around the land for any threats, we began the difficult task of rowing the heavy load through the calm waters.

"I sure hope George got a message to one of our ships," I said between strokes. Nobody responded.

Chapter 35

After only a half hour of rowing, our arms were screaming, and we decided to take a break.

"How far do you think we've gone?" I asked as the boats rocked gently in the water.

"Hard to tell," Jackson replied. "I can't see the shore anymore, so we're a decent ways out, but..."

"Hey, guys," Tank interrupted. "What's that over there?" We all looked to the northwest where he was pointing. I squinted, trying to make out the shapes. Unfortunately there was no moon that night, making things very dark out on the sea. In the distance, I saw a series of lights above the water, probably from a boat of some kind, but it was hard to tell from such a distance.

"That's gotta be it," Jackson declared.

"Are you sure?" Sam said doubtfully. "All I see is a boat."

"It has to be," Jackson insisted. "I can't row much longer." We all agreed and tried to stretch our arms a bit before resuming our trek with renewed hope.

"So, what would you do with the money?" Sam asked once the boats were moving again.

"It's not ours to spend," Tank reminded him.

"I know, I know. But if it was..."

"I'd buy a new house," Jackson declared. "Somewhere in upstate New York—way back in the woods where no one would know I existed. I'd get like fifty acres and build put my house right in the center. It'd be nice and peaceful that way. And I'd have a library full of first editions."

"Not bad," I nodded. "The first thing I'd buy is a ring for my girlfriend."

"And after that?" Sam asked.

"I dunno." I'd never really considered having that much money. The hundred grand I had negotiated with the President seemed like a ridiculous sum. "Maybe I'd buy a baseball team."

"Like George junior," Jackson said.

"Who?" I asked.

"George Bush, the President's son."

"His son's name is George Bush too?"

Jackson laughed. "You don't pay much attention to politics, do you?"

"No, not really."

"Well, the President's son just bought a partial share in the Rangers last year after helping his dad with the campaign," Jackson explained. "It's a good investment from what I understand."

"I'd invest in something more technological," Tank announced.

"Like what? Betamax?" Jackson teased.

"Yeah," Sam jumped in, "you do kinda seem like a Betamax guy."

"Ha ha," Tank replied, "I'll have you know my wife bought me a VHS player when they first came out."

"Well, at least one of you has some sense," Jackson said.

"What would you invest in?" I asked, genuinely curious.

Tank considered for a moment. "Have you heard of this World Wide Web?"

"A little bit," I nodded hesitantly. One of my professors at Iowa State had been real excited about the global network, but I wasn't sure that I fully understood the point of such a system.

"I don't really see it being 'World Wide'," Jackson declared. "I mean it could be useful for a big company I suppose, but most people can't afford to have a computer in their house. And even if they could, what would they need to be able to share documents for?"

"Well, you wouldn't have to mail letters anymore," Tank explained. "You could just send it to the person's computer."

Jackson laughed, "Yeah right. I'm gonna pay for a computer and long distance charges instead of a quarter for a stamp. Do you know how many letters I could send for that kind of money?"

"I mostly just get junk mail anyway," Sam added. "The credit card offers alone would probably fill up my hard drive."

"You're not seeing the bigger picture," Tank argued. "The costs will come down, and the time savings will be enormous."

"I dunno, maybe," Jackson relented. "I guess we'll know in about twenty years, huh?"

While they argued about the potential for invisible connections between computers, I scanned the horizon for the boat we were attempting to reach. I thought the lights looked somewhat closer now, although I couldn't say for sure, but the boat itself was still hard to make out. One of the lights was flashing, and as I watched, I noticed an irregular pattern to it. It looked odd, sometimes flicking on and off very quickly, and other times staying on for nearly a second. I thought perhaps it had a loose wire or something. Then it hit me.

"It's morse code!" I almost shouted.

"What?" Jackson said.

"That flashing light," I insisted, pointing out over the sea. The rowing ceased momentarily as everyone strained to see. I had learned morse code as a kid, mostly just for fun. My friends and I thought it would be cool to be able to talk in code. Of course we were never any good at it in practice; it took too long to refer to the cheat sheet all the time.

"Well, what does it say then?" Sam asked.

"I dunno," I shrugged. "I don't know morse code well enough to read it that quickly."

"I might be able to," Tank said, staring intently at the light. We waited breathlessly as he struggled to work out the interpretation. It took several cycles of the repeating pattern before he was able to piece it together. "It says... run... her... car... no wait, run here... cared..." he paused, frowning at the light.

"Run here cared... what?" Jackson prompted.

"That's it," Tank shrugged. "It just keeps repeating those three words—run, here, cared."

"But that doesn't make any sense," Sam said. "How could you run to a boat? And what is 'cared' supposed to mean?"

"That can't be right," Jackson insisted. "Try it again."

Tank shook his head in frustration and watched the light for several more minutes. I did my best to read the signal as well, but it had been a long time.

"I'm telling you, that's what it says," he insisted. "R-U-N-H-E-R-E-C-A-R-E-D."

It suddenly occurred to me that when we had tried morse code as kids, we had often mixed up letters because of a confusion with where one letter stopped and another started. Two E's (each simply a dot) often were mistaken for an I (two dots). Similarly, an 'IE' (three dots total) might be translated as an 'S'. There was supposed to be a pause after each letter, but it was sometimes hard to interpret.

"That's not what it says," I laughed. Everyone turned to me with questioning looks. "There's no pause between the E and the D," I explained.

"So?" Jackson pressed. I looked to Tank to see if he understood his mistake, but he just frowned, still trying to do the conversion.

"Dot, Dash, Dot, Dot is not E and D," I declared.

"It's an L," Tank said with a sigh.

I nodded. "The message is 'run here Carl'."

Sam smiled broadly. "The boat is talking to me."

Chapter 36

"At least we know where we're heading now," Jackson said. "We'd better get back to rowing."

We returned our oars to the water with renewed vigor. There was light at the end of the tunnel. We simply had to get close enough to signal the boat. They would pick us up and for the first time in several days, we really would be safe. We could probably be in the air by sunup, and it was only a matter of time before I was back in Pennsylvania with Katie, telling her all about...

A loud crack from behind the boat startled me and I jerked my head around to look. In doing so, our boat rocked violently and nearly capsized.

"Calm down!" Tank shouted from the bow. "I don't really feel like swimming right now."

"Sorry. What was that noise?"

"I dunno."

"I do," Sam said grimly. "Stop rowing." I realized suddenly that my oar was still dragging in the water. I quickly lifted it into the air so as not to arrest our progress any more than I already had.

"What's the problem?" Jackson asked. I could now see what Sam had, but Jackson and Tank could not from the fronts of the boats.

"The rope broke," I explained. One of our cargo loads was now floating slowly away at the mercy of the waves.

Jackson sighed. "Alright, who wants to go fix it?"

"I'll do it," I offered. Everyone looked at me in surprise.

"Really? You're volunteering?" Sam asked incredulously.

"Well, you're gonna end up making 'the rookie' do it anyway," I explained.

"That's true," Tank nodded.

"Besides, I like water. I don't mind." Everyone was perfectly happy to let me jump into the dark, unknown sea, and Tank leaned to counter my weight as I dumped myself overboard.

"Hurry up," Jackson said once I was out of the boat. He motioned toward the blinking light in the distance. "We don't want to miss our ride."

The water was not nearly as cool as I had expected. I was pretty sure that my high school swim coach had kept the pool at a lower temperature than this sea was.

"It's pretty nice in here," I joked, doing a leisurely backstroke away from the boat.

"The rope..." Jackson prodded.

"Alright, alright," I moaned, and then under my breath, "We wouldn't want to accidentally have any fun now, would we?" I rolled over to a front crawl and quickly reached the floating gold. There were about two feet of rope still hanging from a ring at the front, which I wrapped around my hand and started pulling. The boat was heavy and moved sluggishly through the water. After progressing only a couple feet, the rope was suddenly jerked from my hand, burning my palm slightly in the process.

"Uh... guys, I think we have a problem," I said, trying to shake the pain out of my hand.

"What?" Sam asked.

"Something is caught on the boat."

"Well, can you get it off?" Jackson said anxiously.

"Maybe. I'll have to go underneath though. I can't see anything from up here."

"Here," Tank said, tossing me the scuba mask and tank. "This might help."

"Thanks." I slipped my arms through the tank's straps and adjusted the mask to fit, before briefly dipping my face under to check for leaks. It seemed to be working fine.

"Take this too," Sam said tossing me a radio headset.

"Is it waterproof?"

He shrugged. "I guess we'll find out."

"How long is this gonna take?" Jackson asked impatiently.

"If you're so worried about the boat leaving, use one of these," Sam said, pulling a flare gun out of a small orange case under his seat.

"Do you think they'll be able to see it this far away?" Tank said doubtfully.

"It's worth a shot. We've got two more that we can save for later just in case."

"Let's do it," Jackson said, retrieving the gun and loading it.

The stream of fire streaked across the sky as I plunged under the surface. Even with the goggles, it was difficult to see in the darkness. I felt the underside of the boat as I worked my way from the front, searching for the problem. About two-thirds of the way back, I felt a large metal hook sticking out of the fiberglass.

"Find anything?" I heard Sam's voice over the headset.

"I looks like we're caught on some fishing lines," I replied.

"That figures. Can you fix it?"

"I think so, but it might take me a minute."

"Alright, keep us updated."

I confirmed that I would, and continued my tactile search of the rest of the hull. It seemed there was just the one hook that was caught underneath, although another one had snagged the tarp up above and a large section now trailed several feet out the back. That hook was easily removed, preventing any further disturbance of the cover.

"One down, one to go," I said cheerily over the radio, as I returned to the one that was dug into the fiberglass. It was nice to finally be doing something I was comfortable with. I could perform much better in the water than I could suspended high above it.

The other hook proved to be a bit more stubborn. After several attempts to wiggle and pull it out, I decided to try a different approach. Reaching into my pants pocket, I retrieved the knife that I had found in the boat house.

"I'm gonna try to cut it loose," I narrated as I began to saw through the twine tied onto the hook.

"Caleb," Sam said with urgency in his voice, "stay quiet for a minute. There's a boat coming."

That sounded like good news to me. "Maybe it's from the ship," I said. "They probably saw the flare."

"Maybe," came the short response. He sounded very nervous, and I wondered what the big deal was. No one knew we were out here except Khalid and even then it would be difficult, if not impossible, to find a few row boats out in the middle of the expansive Red Sea. And then I realized—it would be difficult, if the row boats didn't shoot off flares giving away their position.

I fought the temptation to surface and see what was happening, instead listening intently to the radio. At first, I could hear only the sound of waves lapping on the sides of the rowboats, but then the quiet roar of a small motor appeared. I listened as it got closer and finally turned off altogether.

"Hello there," Jackson called, apparently trying to act friendly.

I knew we were in trouble when the response came back in Arabic. Great, more adventure. The hundred grand I had negotiated for a few days earlier seemed almost laughable now. I was definitely going to ask for a bonus, assuming I got the chance.

I tried to stay as still as possible under the boat as I listened to Sam converse briefly with the men in their native tongue. They sounded very angry and were obviously giving orders. Sam translated for the rest of the group, though I was pretty sure it was mostly intended for me.

"They say they are taking the gold, and we are to get on their boat."

"You mean this little fishing boat right in front of us?" Tank asked. "It's gonna be a little crowded."

Good. They were feeding me information. Now I just had to figure out what to do with it.

"There's only four of them," Jackson said. "I'll bet we could take 'em."

"No," Sam replied. "They all have guns. We just need to do what they say and wait for someone to rescue us." He emphasized the word 'someone', and I knew he was talking about me.

There were more directions given in Arabic, and I heard my partners climbing up onto the fishing boat. It wouldn't take long for them to tie onto the row boats, so I had to act fast.

Trying to minimize my chances of being detected, I swam under the boats in the direction Tank had guided me to. As I cleared the front of the row boats, I could see several lights above the surface, and knew I was on the right track. Soon, a wooden hull came into view. It seemed logical that the men would all be facing toward the row boats, and my friends, so I swam under and cautiously surfaced on the other side.

Floating against the sidewall of the boat, it was very dark. As I had assumed, the lights were all on the opposite side. I felt along the periphery of the hull, moving toward what I thought was the rear. I could hear the men giving more orders to Sam in Arabic as they tossed a line down for him to tie onto the rowboat. I knew I was running out of time. I needed a plan—or at least a way to stay with the fishing boat.

My hand touched something metal as I reached the stern. I felt more closely and realized that it was the propeller for the motor. It occurred to me that this was probably not the best place to be if they decided to start the thing up again. Looking around hastily, I could find nothing to grab onto. I needed some way to stay with the boat once they decided to move on.

I heard footsteps move in my direction and quickly dipped below the surface just before a flashlight came into view above the motor. As I had feared, the propeller was soon spinning away, and the boat began to move. I started to panic. Not only was the boat leaving with my friends, and the gold, but I was going to be stuck out here in the middle of the Red Sea all alone. I needed some way to stay with that boat.

And then it hit me.

Chapter 37

I was disoriented at first as the fiberglass hull collided with my head. The row boat was moving very slowly and the impact was minimal, but my goggles were dislodged momentarily, letting in a rush of water. After the initial shock, I quickly recovered and made a lunging grab for one of the ropes attaching the tarp to the side.

As the boat dragged me slowly through the water, I prayed that the men would not be able to see me. I was mostly concealed under the surface; only my wrist and hand emerged into the air, clutching the rope. Unless a flashlight was shined directly on my hand, it was doubtful that I would be exposed.

I hung alongside the boat for several minutes, formulating a plan. Tank had said there were four men on board and that they had guns. I clearly would have the element of surprise, but I had little in the way of a weapon; I would literally be the man who brought a knife to a gunfight. My plan would have to be smarter than simply boarding the ship and attacking.

I slowly worked my way to the front of the row boat and grasped the ring. There were no people or lights visible at the back of the fishing vessel. They were mostly likely all busy driving and guarding prisoners since they had no reason to suspect danger from behind.

Pulling myself up out of the water a bit, I reached under the tarp and retrieved one of the gold bars. I slipped it into my pocket and moved hand over hand along the rope toward the noisy motor. I began to have second thoughts about my strategy as I approached the spinning propeller, but it was the only workable scenario I could come up with under the conditions. With a sigh, I hefted the block of gold into the air and threw it sharply at the propeller.

The effect was as intended. Two of the spinning blades were bent oddly and wedged up against the side of the motor's housing. The propeller wrenched to a halt and made several loud popping noises as it struggled against itself. Loud Arabic could be heard from on board as the boat came to a quick stop, and I hastily withdrew into the water to wait.

From several feet under the surface, I couldn't see what was happening above me at the back of the boat, but I did see a light appear and assumed it was someone inspecting the damaged motor. There were muffled voices and then another light appeared next to the first. I fingered the knife in my pocket but resisted the urge to take it out. I couldn't risk alerting the others to my presence just yet. The lights disappeared again, and I knew it was only a matter of time until...

The water in front of me erupted in a flurry of dark bubbles when the man jumped in. He was closer than I had expected, which worked to my advantage as I grabbed his ankle and swam straight down as hard as I could. It took a second for him to react, and when he did I nearly lost my grip. He kicked furiously and thrashed his body around, clearly panicking.

I wondered if he even knew what had a hold of him. I also wondered how far down I would need to go. I was counting on the fact that most people exhaled after jumping into the water, so he would have a limited supply of air. He would also most likely have breathed in a healthy dose of sea water in his initial panic.

My predictions must have been accurate, because it didn't take long for his struggle to diminish. His kicks became further apart and less violent. I stopped my descent and reversed direction, dragging his ankle back toward the surface and turning him upside down. Then I released the disoriented man with no hope for returning to the boat.

255

With the deed done, my departure was hurried; I had little desire to see the result of my actions. I knew it had to be done, and it was certainly justified, but that didn't make me feel any better about it. I pushed the guilt to the side and focused on saving my friends.

As I neared the surface, the dark bottom of the boat came into view once more. I glanced briefly toward the stern and the broken propeller, and saw a pair of lights dancing on the water. As expected, the man's mysterious disappearance had warranted an investigation by the others.

I moved several feet to the side of the boat and gently lifted my head out of the water, being careful not to make too much noise. I could see the three remaining captors arguing at the back of the boat as they searched the water with their flashlights. This was the best chance I would have.

I returned to the protection of the dark water once again and swam quickly to the bow. It was a tall boat, and I started to think I wouldn't be able to reach over the side. I could feel myself begin to panic. My plan had worked so perfectly so far; surely I wasn't going to fail now. I tried to stay calm and find a solution. Maybe the other side would yield better results.

I quickly moved around the front of the boat, but the other side looked exactly the same. I considered trying to jump, as much as one can when treading water, but I knew that would create too much noise. I needed a new approach and decided to submerge once again.

As I sunk under the water, I saw it—just under the surface on the side of the boat was a hole with a screw on cap. It was probably a port for letting water into a live well, but it would work perfectly as a foothold. I emerged from the sea once again and listened carefully. Several voices were still talking loudly at the back of the boat.

Lifting my foot up onto the cap and grasping the angled front of the boat with one hand, I was able to swing my other hand up high enough to grip the top of the railing. From there, I pulled myself into a standing position, supported by my improvised foothold. With a deep breath, I raised my head slowly above the railing and surveyed the scene.

Chapter 38

Sam, Tank, and Jackson were crowded into the front of the boat, not more than three feet from where I stood. They seemed to be okay physically, although clearly uncomfortable. Their wrists and ankles had been bound with thick ropes, and the two ropes were hooked together with a large carabineer, forcing them to lean forward and hold their hands at their feet at all times.

Two of the remaining kidnappers stood on either side of the rear of the boat with flashlights, still searching the water for any sign of their partner. The third hung over the edge, attempting to assess the damage to the propeller. Not surprisingly, he was hesitant to jump in for a closer look.

Removing the knife from my pants pocket, I tapped gently on the railing, trying to err on the side of too quiet. I was apparently successful in my error, as no one on board appeared to hear anything. I tapped again, slightly louder this time, and Jackson lifted his head as if something had arrested his attention. A quick click of the tongue, and he turned around quizzically. His eyes lit up when he saw me, and his mouth opened to speak. He was about to ruin everything. I shook my head and held a finger to my lips, and he quickly closed his mouth, realizing his mistake.

I motioned toward him with the knife and he nodded his understanding. This was going to be the tricky part. Flipping it around, I grabbed the blade and carefully tossed it into his lap, handle first. It landed exactly as intended, with the rubber taking the brunt of the force. By now, Tank was also aware of my presence and was smiling broadly at me. I pointed to myself and to the back of the boat and he seemed to get the picture.

Jackson started cutting through his ropes, and I returned to the water and swam quickly under the kidnappers above to the rowboat full of gold. I made sure to stay several feet deep in order to avoid the flashlights searching for signs of life. We had been drifting now for several minutes, and the row boat was turned sideways, facing perpendicular to the threat less than twenty feet away. I was pleasantly surprised by this discovery and felt emboldened.

Surfacing behind the gold, I watched the commotion on the fishing boat. The captors had now abandoned the search for their comrade and were focusing on the broken motor. They gave no indications that they were aware of what was happening behind them in the bow. I decided to sit tight and give the guys another minute to remove their restraints. It would do me no good to jump the gun.

My hand was forced several seconds later, however, as the man hanging over the rear of the boat pushed himself back up onto the deck and turned to face the front. In a matter of seconds, he would become aware of the escape in progress. Pulling myself up out of the water as much as I could, I waved one arm over my head.

"Looking for me?" I shouted, making as much of a commotion as possible. Almost immediately, several lights were trained on my face. I watched as all the men's expressions changed from surprise to anger and three AK-47 barrels were aimed in my direction. I dipped quickly beneath the water and swung my legs up to the surface. As bullets littered the opposite side of the boat, I did a semi-leisurely back float, protected by the pile of gold bars that deflected every shot.

Regardless of the quality of my protection, I was scared out of my mind. I knew the gold would shield me, but I wasn't expecting it to be so loud. It sounded like the boat was exploding right next to me. But the noise was as brief as it was loud. After several seconds, the shooting stopped and was replaced by shouts, a loud splash, and finally two more single shots. I lay perfectly still, afraid to look, until at length I heard Jackson's voice.

"Caleb, you okay?" he hollered.

I slowly lifted my head up just enough to peek over the pile of gold. Jackson and Tank were standing at the back of the boat waving at me.

"Where's Sam?" I called. A head poked up over the railing as he stood. He had apparently been kneeling or sitting on the deck, but looked to be okay. I swam back to the boat, relieved that I didn't have to be quiet anymore.

Chapter 39

The small inflatable raft bounced rhythmically in the waves as we sped across the Red Sea. The fishing boat's motor was out of commission, but the radio had worked beautifully, and in a matter of minutes, a group of Sailors were transporting us and the gold to the protection of a U.S. Navy destroyer. Sitting next to someone who had an actual gun—and knew how to use it—I felt it was finally safe to say that we were going to survive our little ordeal, although I knew we were probably still being pursued by unseen threats.

I realized this must have been how the Israelites felt as they crossed the same body of water thousands of years earlier while being chased down by the Egyptians. Of course, their trip had been a bit more impressive than an inflatable raft with a motor strapped on back. I searched the sky, hoping for a pillar of fire, but found only stars.

I started to relax as the destroyer came into view again. It seemed so small off in the distance, just a dark silhouette under the new moon sky. Then as we neared the giant ship, I thought it was never going to stop growing. I was marveling at the incredible engineering feat of making something that large seaworthy, when it happened.

Something in the sky above the ship caught my eye. I glanced up just in time to watch a meteor streak across the dark expanse above. I thought my eyes were playing tricks on me at first, as the flaming rock crossed directly through the three stars of Orion's belt. The bright trail, combined with the trio of stars, left a temporary image on my retina that looked peculiarly like a fiery column, and I knew then that we would make it back home okay.

Once on board, we were whisked to the helm where the Captain, a large man with a strong southern accent and a touch of gray hair, waited for us.

"I don't know who you boys are, but somebody must think you're important," he retorted as we stepped through the open doorway.

"Yes, sir," Jackson said, ignoring the Captain's obvious curiosity about our presence in the region.

"Thanks for the ride," Tank added.

The Captain waited for a moment, and then realized that we weren't offering any details. "Well, whatever you were doing, it must have been important. The President called me directly and asked me to come pick you up." He studied us for a minute, still hoping we'd fill him in. We gave nothing, and he continued. "Luckily, we were in the area already, so it didn't take us too long to get here."

"Why were you in the area?" Tank asked.

"Flexing our muscles for Saddam, of course," the Captain said, as if the answer was obvious. Our faces must have indicated that we were naïve to the situation. "Where have you boys been all day?"

"We were... otherwise engaged," I offered.

"Well, earlier today Iraqi military troops moved into Kuwait. The leaders of several nations are calling for a special session of the U.N. to be convened to condemn the action and discuss possible sanctions and/or military action if he does not withdraw immediately."

We exchanged weary glances, and Jackson spoke first, "So, Saddam is removing his troops then."

"Not yet," the Captain explained. "So far he's refusing to talk to anyone. But don't worry, I'm sure he wouldn't risk going to war with the United Nations over a little country like Kuwait. What could they have that he would want?"

"Yeah... I'm sure you're right," I managed, and then changed the subject. "Do you think we could get some clean clothes and a shower, Captain? I've got sand in places I didn't even know existed."

"Yes, of course," he replied, directing us through a doorway. "Go right ahead. You've got about an hour until the transport chopper arrives."

"Thanks."

Chapter 40

"So, you're sure you're not mad?" I asked Katie for the tenth time.

"No, I'm not mad," she answered, though I still doubted it. "I'm just glad to hear you're okay."

"I am," I assured her. The conversation had gone much better than I'd expected, and her reaction solidified both my plans to join the committee and to spend my pay on an engagement ring. "And I promise, I'll explain everything later tonight, but I need to get going right now."

"Okay," she sighed. "You'll be at my place at eight?"

I confirmed that I would and said my goodbyes before hanging up the car phone. It felt strange to be back in Washington. As I rode through the crowded streets in the back of another black Lincoln, I did the math in my head and realized it had been less than seventy-two hours since I had first arrived at the White House, though it felt like ages ago. I had been around the world and back in that time.

Agent Smith drove slowly up the long drive to the President's home, and I was surprised to find that I felt completely at ease. Going to the White House to see the most powerful man in the free world now seemed like a natural thing to do. I was no longer nervous. I guess that's what happens when you're shot at. Or maybe it was the thrill of catching the bad guy and recovering nearly a billion dollars worth of gold. Of course, in the back of my mind there was still that nagging feeling that we may have also triggered an international incident.

Only time would tell what would come of Saddam's invasion of Kuwait, although I could say for sure that he was not going to find his missing gold.

Author's Note

The preceding story was a work of fiction. I have no evidence to support, nor do I believe, that Adolf Hitler or the Nazi Party was in control of Cuba, South Africa, Iraq, or Al Qaeda. I also do not claim that the United States government, nor President George Bush, allowed Iraq to invade Kuwait looking for gold that we stole from Saddam Hussein, or that 'The Committee' actually exists.

If, however, at some point in the future any of these crazy ideas somehow turn out to be true, I'll gladly take the credit as the person who figured it all out.

CPSIA information can be obtained
at www.ICGtesting.com
Printed in the USA
BVHW052150220223
659058BV00007B/40